Heart's a Mess

Liz Ashlee

Heart's a Mess
Copyright © 2020 Liz Ashlee
All rights reserved.

ISBN: (ebook): 978-1-949931-91-4
(print): 978-1-949931-92-1

Inkspell Publishing
207 Moonglow Circle #101
Murrells Inlet, SC 29576

Edited By Yezanira Yenecia
Cover Art By Najla Qamber

For my adorable, dorky, smart, weird, and cute dog-daughter,
Hero.

CHAPTER 1

John

"Tell me, my friends, who here has opened their heart to God and prayed for Him to offer His hand to help? I know, I *know* we all have seen His graciousness—we have all *witnessed* His kindness. Let us each pray, in His heavenly spirit, that He will appear here with us today as we heal another soul," Reverend Ezra Abel bellows into his microphone, slamming his palm against his podium for emphasis. "Now, who of us needs His guidance today?"

He steps from behind the podium, holding one arm open as if presenting his body as some sort of stand-in for God. I'm sure there is a God, but Ezra Abel's church is the devil's territory. In his khaki pants and navy-colored suit coat, he looks unassuming, but his salt and peppered hair is too gelled, his unemotional, slate eyes too quick, and jaw too stern. He's a predator dressed up as a good guy. Nobody, except for me, can see the truth in his heartless ways.

The woman next to me nearly throws herself into the row of people ahead of us—which wouldn't be too disastrous, considering that row is just as frantic. The man

1

beside me has already elbowed me in the head and rib cage, not even bothering to apologize. There's not a single person in the audience—other than me—who wouldn't kiss at the man's bare feet just because he's in their presence. I'd rather set myself on fire and wrestle with the devil than approach Ezra Abel with anything other than hate.

"Now, now," he says, offering a grin that shows his too white, too sharp teeth. "Let's not be greedy. We all know our God would not want that of us. All He wants is for everyone to show Him support and love—to give Him what He has given to you."

An intrinsic message—when the hat comes around, put in money or a check. I know from personal experience the higher the check, the more likely you'll be chosen to be healed.

He holds his hand up to his head, careful not to mess up his grooming. That will come later—it always does. "Bea Pierce, the Lord Jesus has asked for your audience. Please join me in His presence."

The crowd becomes quiet as a woman several rows ahead stands and begins making her way toward the aisle. People let her through easily but not without patting her on the shoulder or hugging her. For these people, she's basically a lottery winner.

The audience sits down in a wave, eyes glued to Ezra Abel. A chunk of me wants to scream at them to open their eyes and ears—but there's no use. They probably believe Ezra created the ground they walk on.

As the woman is walking up the aisle to the podium, she develops a limp and her shoulders hunch over, her arms wrapping around her waist. As she disappears further into herself, I can't help thinking she's getting into character.

Honestly, she's probably not a character Ezra or his bazaar family created—she's probably doing this all on her own. The natural instinct is to play the big-fish game, where you make your problems seem worse than they are. I doubt it's on purpose; it's probably just a way to feel more important—an opportunity to monopolize the spotlight.

As Bea takes the stage, the lights closest to Ezra brighten. He's always careful in his stage presence, but I've seen his wife and daughter motioning to the wall on the right. There's a huge picture of their crazed family, larger than the painting of Jesus on the opposite wall. I'll bet there's a camera hidden near there, someone on the other end waiting for stage direction. Ezra doesn't need lighting to make his presence known, but it does make him seem larger than life.

"Please stand beside me, child," he says, even though Bea's got a decade or so on him. She immediately takes the spot next to him. He faces her, imposing on her space. "Are you, Bea Pierce, willing to accept God into your heart? Are you willing to sacrifice all for Him and forever be His servant to save your soul and your life?"

He holds the microphone out. Every time this part comes, I have to pretend to scratch at my chin, or else I'll roar with laughter. If you read between the lines, it sounds as though he's more concerned with gathering an army than filling a church.

Not that anybody else ever notices.

"I'll serve God, but I'll also serve you eternally."

He purses his lips as if trying to hold back his emotions, but then gives in and places his palm flat against her cheek. What an actor.

"Then you're ready to accept God's solutions," he tells her.

He motions for his wife, Michelle, and daughter, Prudence, to join him on stage. His wife has always seemed enthralled by Ezra's power, but also as though she has no other choice than to go along with it. Her crystal eyes are always bleary and never focused, and she's always wearing a haunting smile. Her mass of tight blonde curls is pulled up into a ponytail. She also has a strange affinity for floor-length dresses, which makes her resemble an extra for a horror movie.

Unlike Michelle, Prudence is more than physically here—she's enjoying every second of it, too. My research puts her at about seventeen, which is old enough for her to already be a cruel human being. There's something to be said about the glee in her dark brown eyes when somebody down on their luck walks onto that stage. She's the type to feed on misery. She's wearing a pair of corduroy pants with a cream sweater, her light brown hair perfectly styled. Seventeen or not, she's in line to be a Stepford wife.

Michelle and Prudence take their usual positions beside Bea. They're there in case something hazardous happens. I learned that the hard way when they tried to heal my father and failed.

My dad was so sick, he could not walk, let alone stand. However, this was against the façade Ezra wanted to present. He asked two parishioners to hold my father up while he healed him. He humiliated a dying man—treated my dad as though this entire thing was anything other than fake. But I'm not here for my dad, I'm here *because* of him. None of this is about revenge, it's about stopping Ezra before he hurts more people.

"Bea, please tell us all what ails you so we can know what our gift from God will be."

John Smith, Sr., he had said during my dad's healing, *your family has pleaded with me to heal you of your ALS, and I will use my hand—directly touched by Gods—to do so.*

Prudence offers Bea another microphone. Bea takes it, face twisting into a grimace as she prepares her words. "My arthritis is so bad I can hardly walk. All I want is to be able to stand straight and sleep through the night. This pain is too heavy to carry."

"The Lord Jesus doesn't want you to carry it," Ezra tells her. If this ordeal ended here, this would all be perfectly acceptable. This is what faith healing should be—

a reminder you are never alone.

Michelle hands Ezra his bible and he starts searching for a passage he undoubtedly already marked. By seemingly happening upon it, he's playing into the narrative of the miracle. He begins reading aloud, his voice growing louder and deeper. He certainly emphasizes words—ones that shouldn't be emphasized, which makes him indecipherable. But the man has a presence like no other. He knows how to become the only voice in the room that matters—to isolate every single person and grip their attention.

When he finishes, he closes the bible. People flinch at the sudden noise in the silence following his recitation. The woman beside me, who's all elbows, is on the edge of her seat.

He places his hands on Bea's shoulders. "Heavenly Father, please help relieve this woman of her suffering. She is your faithful servant." His voice is a building murmur. Bea leans her head back, not to look toward Heaven but toward Ezra. "Let her love for you, Lord, heal her. Your blood courses through her veins—through mine—ours. We exist to serve you and ask for you to serve us in the name of Bea."

The lights grow brighter. Another organized tactic. It probably feels similar to the light of God to the parishioners, but it feels more like an alien abduction to me.

"God is here; can you feel Him?" Ezra asks. Regardless of whether he's asking Bea or the parishioners, the entire church answers with a "yes." "God is here with us—in us—to save us all by helping Bea. Through my hands, Bea, you will be healed."

He pushes at her shoulders with enough force that she stumbles back two short steps. Her body seems to lurch forward, making her seem as if she's folded into herself. Ezra's audience is completely still, completely quiet, waiting. I'm sure none of them are thinking what I am:

what if he just made her worse? Her body seems to be more tortured than it was before. He pushed her, for love of God. How is that supposed to help her?"

Bea slowly straightens, revealing a face full of joy.

"Bea…" Ezra says, "How do you feel?"

"I feel healed!" she declares.

The whole church erupts in cheers. It's hard to tell the parishioners apart—it's just a faceless group of followers who are feeding off each other.

I rub at my temple, fighting the urge to throw my notebook at them and yell until my voice is hoarse. Ezra went through this same sermon, almost verbatim, during Dad's healing.

Please step aside so we can see the glory of God.

Back when it was my dad being healed, not Bea, the parishioners had stepped aside at Ezra's cue, letting go of him. I knew in an instant that the healing hadn't worked. Pain and terror twisted my father's expression into the face of someone who was already a ghost of a man. Then he fell—fell so hard the church instantly went silent, and his fall echoed for what felt like days.

When his skin brushed against the stage floor, it tore and blood began to flood the area around him. He was in so much pain, he passed out.

To my whole family's horror, the moment only worsened when Ezra pointed his menacing finger in my dad's direction.

You cannot be healed. You have not allowed God into your heart. You will go to hell.

Bea's voice removes me from the past. Thank God I haven't had to witness something as what happened to my dad again.

"Thank you, Ezra," she says, then kneels—throwing a grin toward the crowd—to kiss his hand. No one notices she isn't thanking the big guy upstairs.

Ezra pats her head as if she were a child and says

something to her that no one else can hear, before stepping around her and holding his arms up similar to a ring leader in the grand finale. Behind him, Bea exits back off the stage. She is walking perfectly straight, although slower than I'd imagine someone who is "healed" might walk. Instead, it's as if her mind is telling her something that her body isn't.

I don't think false confidence or mind over matter are entries in the bible, although Ezra brandishes them like weapons.

When Ezra faces us all, he's toting a deadly sin—pride. Maybe he believes he did heal her—not God. *Him.*

"The Lord Jesus will always answer our call so long as we hold our faith in God. As long as I lead this church, God will be in our audience. I promise you all that He will heal and help those who have opened their heart to our church."

And their wallets.

CHAPTER 2

Kinley

"Did you see him? He was here again," my father—Ezra, as he prefers me to call him—says to us as we clean the church. He's counting the donations with his greedy hands. The last parishioner left ten minutes ago, allowing Prudence to lock the doors and for me to come out of my "effects" room.

Michelle nods absently. I'm not sure if it's the pills or her blindness from Ezra's shine, but she's extra spacey today. She nearly didn't make it on stage because it was as if she forgot how to walk. Ezra was furious with her, even though he's the one who encourages her to take another pill whenever he doesn't want to deal with her.

He's not looking for an actual answer. Instead, he slams his hand against a dollar bill to flatten it, his nostrils flaring. "Same row, same seat, with that damn notebook of his, writing in it like he's a reporter. He won't get a goddamn thing out of us. There ain't nothing illegal about practicing religion."

"No, Daddy, there's not," Prudence offers.

"Don't speak when you've not been spoken to,

9

Prudence," he growls.

Prudence sputters and returns to stacking the bibles. Each has a Church of Life sticker on it. Years ago, when Prudence and I put those on, she'd hated Ezra, too. But now she's another one of his followers—hanging on his every word and doing her best to impress him. She knows it's all fake—that he's fake—but I think she would easily believe him if he said it was all real. She wouldn't even blink.

"I swear if he makes one false move against us …" Ezra continues, trailing off and shaking his head. The vein in his neck is pulsing with fury. He's excellent at faking emotions around everyone else, but he doesn't try to around us. We get the brunt of it all. "I will not let him burn what I've built."

What he's built? Goodness, it's the truth, even though he stole the church from its original minister. None of this would exist without his cruel ingenuity. I'm currently sorting through "Letters to God" he tells parishioners to write when they need help, but we only use them as a tool. Nobody even questions how we know all their problems—they don't even suspect we read the letters and use them as information sources. He built trust with these people by showing interest, even though he wasn't necessarily *taking* an interest. He built this congregation by putting on a show no one could resist. He built our income through "donations" and deep pockets with big problems. He built this church on the framework of a con scheme.

Everything about us—including my and my sister's adoption—is a carefully-engineered move in a never-ending chess game.

"I thought for sure we'd gotten rid of him by sending Officer Aims to talk to him," he grumbles.

He sent Officer Aims? My heart slams on the breaks, coming to an abrupt and painful halt. Officer Aims is one of Ezra's original followers but also the creepiest. The man never shows any emotion and has arms that could lift a car—intimidating is too soft of a word to describe him. Even though he made an oath to protect and serve, the only person he truly serves is Ezra. He's corrupt—willing to scare away anyone who crosses the church, namely Ezra.

I didn't think the man Ezra's been so worried about warrants a visit from Aims. Some of the people Ezra's feared have just been curious or shy or just wanted to wait before becoming a member. We don't even know if he's doing anything against us, let alone what his real name is, because he just puts J.S. in the attendance book each week.

I could measure my lifetime in the number of people Ezra has found suspicious. He seems to discover a new obsession every time he rids himself of another. All of the people he thinks are against him usually end up disappearing—whether it is because they've lost interest, he's scared them off, or he's done something else, I never know. I remember him once thinking that an elderly woman was trying to turn the church against him—really, she was just an extreme gossiper—so he ended up pulling strings to have her committed to a nursing home facility. There have been countless others who have mysteriously been sent to jail, come upon illnesses, or been hospitalized. This is often where Ezra enlists Aims as his heavy.

J.S. appeared on Ezra's radar slowly, as most do. He noticed the odd initialing in the books rather than putting a full name, then that he never offered money to the till (a high crime in his court), and that he often didn't cheer and chant like the other parishioners.

Those were only small occurrences—things Ezra noted as suspicious but probably wrote off because J.S. was new. It takes some longer than others to fall under Ezra's spell. But I think that Ezra's deciding factor about J.S. happened last weekend.

On occasion, Ezra will take time to walk down each aisle to offer individual congregates a direct phrase from

God. These are often repeated, counterfeit affirmations or warnings that don't relate to anyone—*The Lord has his hand on your shoulder. You will find you your way. Things will work out* …

People rarely, if ever, turn this down. Whether they follow Ezra's word or not, it is hard not to see the magic of the moment. The room is wrapped up in hope and happiness and promise. How do you deny yourself that?

J.S. did.

I was watching Ezra because he prefers the spotlight to follow him when he does this. When he made it to J.S.'s row and eventually brought his hand up to touch J.S.'s shoulder, J.S. dodged away from him. Even though I had witnessed this, it still seemed impossible. No one ever rejected Ezra.

They stared at each other for a moment, but not long enough for anyone who isn't accustomed to the cues that Ezra is angry to notice it. His fists were balled, his cheeks were hollowed, and his chin was raised.

But so were J.S.'s. When J.S. turned his back toward him and weaved his way out of the crowd—rejecting Ezra entirely.

"We need to figure out who he is," he continues. There's a glint in his eyes that makes me uncomfortable—especially because he's looking right at Prudence. Ever since she turned seventeen, he's been weaponizing her as a siren. "Prudence, what do you think about befriending him?"

He means more than befriending, of course; he's disgusting. But what feels even worse is that he's taking advantage of Prudence. She *wants* to do this, and instead of playing the role of father, he's going to let her.

She grins. "I'd love to."

"Whatever you do, make sure there's evidence," he says as if she needs reminding.

Blackmail. My stomach turns over. Good or bad, J.S. is going to be put in a bait trap. If Prudence finds out he's against us, she'll do her best to sway his opinion. If that doesn't work, she'll lead him to believe she's older and put him in a position that can potentially ruin him.

But just because he's against the church doesn't mean he's the villain.

"No," I say, some of the letters falling to the floor.

Everybody looks over at me as if they just remembered I exist. Before the Church of Life, I used to be the favorite. "You're vulnerable," Ezra would say, meaning that people were more willing to give to the vulnerable. Michelle would matt my hair, then pull it half up into a ponytail so the burn on my cheek, ear, and neck would be prominent. My clothes always came from thrift stores that she would also leave out in the elements to make them look *authentic*. They put me on busy street corners, where I would beg for money—*My family is hungry, please help.* That stopped when a good Samaritan tried to take me to a children's home.

Nothing they made me do mattered, because as long as I did what they wanted, they'd foster Prudence, too. But then they started the church, Prudence started to change and stopped caring, and they didn't want their unhealable, broken daughter in the public eye.

Ezra looks like he's about to say his "do not speak" mantra, but I open my mouth before he can. Words tumble out. "I'll do it—I'll befriend him. Prudence can't because he's seen her. There's no way he's going to *trust* her, let alone be convinced of anything. But if I go, he won't know me. I'm a complete stranger, and that will—"

"Stop talking, Kinley, and let me think," he says, cutting me off. He runs his hand through his messy hair. Throughout the service it always goes from perfect to, well, chaos. He pulls on the ends, scrutinizing me. "What about your face?"

"Oh, honey," Michelle says, voice faint, "people love ugly nowadays."

Reflexes order me to touch the rough, always-warm

scar, but I keep my hands at my side.

Ezra nods, then stands straight. "That's what you will do, then—and you will do it right," he orders. "I'll call Aims and find out what he knows."

As soon as Ezra's left to go to his office, the atmosphere electrifies in the most painful way. My sister, who suddenly became the forgotten one, stomps toward me, her nostrils flaring and her cheeks blood red.

"What are you doing?" she demands. "That was *my* job—how dare you take it away from me!"

I glance over at Michelle, who's happily humming to herself while she takes up counting the money.

I keep my voice low, just in case. "You're too young, Prudence."

"That's never mattered before!"

"I know, which is why it's stopping *now,*" I say. "I'm doing this out of your best interest."

Her glossy lips purse as she places her hands on her hips. "You don't know what you're doing. You don't understand anymore."

Standing face to face, it feels as though I don't understand *her* anymore. But I can't think that way. Somewhere underneath all of Ezra's brainwashing, she's still the giggly little girl who was always scraping her knees and dreaming about chocolate palaces.

"Please let me do this," I say.

She looks over my shoulder, at the door Ezra went out. "There's nothing I can do about it; Daddy already gave the job to you."

#

He—J.S.—eats at a diner every day called Velma's Vittles.

Velma's is one of a few storefronts in a busy, historic district of a town three counties away from the church. Each store has its own distinct look, but Velma's stands out with its teal-colored paneling around the doors and wall-to-ceiling windows. The second-floor exterior is white-bricked, with yellow flowers in the window boxes. Since it's the far most building in the line, there's greenery growing up one part of the wall and onto a yellow canvas overhang. The place is homey—unique.

I've been trying to avoid eye contact with the alley next to it, which leads to a small parking lot, where Officer Aims tried to scare him off with his taser. I didn't want or need to know this, but Ezra never tries to spare our feelings.

Whether it's the cold chill in the air or my nerves, I bundle down into my peacoat. I've been trying to talk myself into walking across the street and into the diner for about ten minutes now, but I can't seem to find the courage. I even pushed the street light button, thinking *this* will be the time, and then I freeze.

I haven't talked to anyone outside of my family in years—probably since Ezra put me on house arrest for my "disfiguration." I don't even know how to approach this man, let alone talk him down from his potential DEFCON 5 mission against my family.

My sister tried giving me a makeover because she lives a world where being pretty gets things done. She didn't do it out of love as much as she did it because it was a demand from Ezra to make me presentable. All the makeup and hair products made me feel more false—as if I was back on the corner begging for money, only instead of being made down, I was being made up. So, I got off at another bus stop and washed my face completely, then pulled half my hair up. The truth is, I don't care about the scar on my face. It's my family that's self-conscious about it. I also changed out of my sister's pick for an outfit—all pearls and flowers—and into a fluffy white sweater with tights.

If I'm going to accomplish anything, I'll do it as myself. There's enough falsities in my life as it is, I don't need to be fake, too.

"Do you have agyrophobia?"

I blink multiple times, then look from the diner where J.S. *should* be and up at where he *actually* is, which is beside me. I would recognize him anywhere, and not just because my dad's been having me keep a camera on him during our services. It's just that he's the only person who's ever stepped foot into the Church of Life and seemed authentic.

He has thick eyebrows that are always so expressive, even when the rest of his face is impassive. Below them are warm, brown, puppy-dog eyes that seem both playful and mindful. His dark, dirty blond hair is usually short. I've noticed he always scratches at a spot behind his ear whenever he's listening closely to Ezra. He doesn't smile a lot in church, but when he does, it's bright and turns my mind inside out, showing off the dimples in his cheeks and his wolfishly sharp teeth. Whenever someone was at the church with a truly bad illness, he would always take extra time to talk to them—offering his kind grin.

"E-e-e-xcuse m-m-me?" I ask, stuttering.

"It's a fear of crossing the street." He offers me that grin as he holds up his phone. "I looked it up before I walked over here. Guess I don't seem as smart now, huh?"

"No," I say, then quickly shake my head. "I mean, yes. I'm sorry, I'm just—"

"It's the hyperthermia kicking in, isn't it?"

"It's hypothermia," I correct, offering him a small, unconfident smile.

He chuckles. "Guess I should've looked that up, too."

In person, he seems warm and inviting, nothing like the evil disruptor Ezra portrays him as. Not that *evil* is the word I would ever use to describe him. He's just blank, critical, an onlooker.

That's not evil. Evilness is a disease that spreads darkness throughout your mind, body, and soul. Just because you do or don't follow, Ezra Abel can't be the deciding factor as to whether your soul will be saved. Not when Ezra is veritably the bad one.

"Not to sound stalkerish, but you've been standing out here for a while," John prompts, rubbing his gloved hands together.

He wasn't inside? I bury my chin in my pink scarf, using the cold as an excuse not to answer automatically. "I was waiting for my sister."

"You couldn't do that inside the diner?" he asks, but then shakes his head. "Sorry, I'm too curious for my own good." He turns around and points at the recently restored apartments above the string of stores opposite the diner. "My window's up there, and I have a dog who's even more curious than I am. She's been barking at you since you started standing there."

I glance back, looking up at the windows for the dog, but I don't see her. I think I might hear her barking somewhere, but it could just be the cold air howling against my ears.

"It's not just you. She barks at everyone," he says. "You're not that special." He tries to say that with a blank expression but ends up smirking. I fight not to touch my own face. *He's not referencing my scar, is he?* Prudence's words echo in my mind, saying dysfunctional is the in-style. I never cared about my scars, but J.S. has me more self-conscious than I've ever been. He's a job given to me by Ezra, so my face, my relationship to Ezra—anything—can ruin this entirely.

But he hasn't looked at my burn once. With that in mind, I try to at least show a smidgeon of personality. That's harder than it sounds because I haven't shown any personality since before my adoption.

"I'm sure your neighbors must love you," I say.

He chuckles. "I've had two warnings in the last month. All of it's eased over by earning my way into their stomachs." He steps closer to me as a car barrels in front of us, ignoring the twenty-miles per hour speed limit.

"How about I treat you to a coffee? At least you might be thawed by the time your sister gets here."

"Okay," I say. My inner voices are saying everything but "okay." In theory, this all seemed doable, but I don't have Prudence's confidence. However, I started this, and I can't just stop.

We walk across the street, side by side. It's weird because Ezra always leads people, whether it's by being in front of them or by putting his hand on their back. It's as if he always has to be in control.

I don't think I've ever been around a man other than Ezra to know how they should and shouldn't act. Growing up, Ezra wouldn't even let us watch movies. Instead, he filled our time with new schemes and made us transcribe his sermons. The only real taste of pop culture either of us had was Sundays at church. Prudence, of course, gained more experience from that because she was actually allowed to interact with the congregation. She was even allowed to date one boy when she was fifteen, but only because he was the son of an influential man on the city council and Ezra needed zoning for an old-time Church Revival.

J.S. jogs ahead slightly to open the door for me, hunched over from the cold.

"Thank you," I breathe as I cross the threshold between chilly winter winds and heat.

The bell *dings* as he steps inside and closes the door behind him. There isn't a lot of space for him to maneuver, because I'm too busy trying to take in my surroundings. The walls are covered with pictures, both new and old, of different customers, along with tons of little signs and wall art. One of the walls has an ornate, brass clock with flowers painted on the face. The room smells heavenly, like chicken noodle soup. This isn't only a diner, it's a microcosm for small-town eateries.

"John, there you are!"

So, John is his first name. It fits him. Simple, familiar.

The woman who spoke passes by us with a half-empty coffee pot. She's older, blonde hair turning gray at the roots, but her posture is straighter than mine, and she moves faster than anyone I've ever seen.

"I know, I know, I'm late, Tonnie. But I was rescuing—" John starts.

"Kinley," I provide.

"Kinley," he repeats slowly, my name sounding mystical coming from his lips. His country accent reminds me of soft cotton—soothing and warm. "I had to save Kinley from evolving into a polar bear."

"Aren't you a regular knight," Tonnie says, although her tone is more mocking than admiring. "Are you eating together or separately?"

"Together, and I'm paying," he tells her.

"Wow, saved *and* fed." Tonnie laughs.

"Actually, we're just getting coffee. Her sister's coming later."

I hold up my phone, hoping nobody notices I haven't looked at it. "She just canceled on me."

"All right, so we are eating."

Tonnie leads us back to a booth with dark green seats and an overhanging light with a stained glass aesthetic. "I shouldn't be joking, considering this is the first time you haven't gone straight to a booth and unloaded that backpack of yours. We all need saving from that Goliath."

John rolls his eyes as he sits down. "I'll have you know, I didn't even bring it today."

"I see that," she says. "A good thing, or else Kinley might go running off."

She takes our drink orders and then leaves us to look over the menu. I should've done more reconnaissance before coming here. I have no idea what type of food is sold here or what's good.

Luckily, John's too busy paying attention to his menu. I eventually settle on the tuna salad sandwich, while John picks a bowl of chili with a grilled cheese sandwich. Once

Tonnie's walked away with our order, he sets his forearms on the table and leans in.

"You haven't been here before, have you?"

"No," I say. "How'd you guess?"

He motions vaguely at the inside of the restaurant. "Because you stopped when we came in. This place is a lot to take in at first. Velma, Tonnie's sister, wanted a place where everybody had something that they could relate to. Then she went overboard on the idea."

"It is a little much," I agree. "But I do like it. I like that there are just so many … options to look at."

"Options, yeah, I never thought about it that way."

"So I guess you're a regular?" I already know, obviously.

"Let's put it this way: if I didn't show up, they'd probably notify the police." He scratches his chin and points up at a black and white photo directly over the booth. A very young Tonnie and a woman who looks almost identical to her are standing beside a little boy. "Velma was my dad's step-mom. She often said my dad was her first employee. He bussed tables."

I note that in my mind. If I don't get any more information today, at least I might be able to track John's history by looking into Tonnie and Velma. Ezra suspects he's a journalist, which should make it even easier to narrow down exactly who he is and find out his motives.

"She's passed, isn't she?"

"Yeah, a couple of years ago."

"I'm very sorry." I try to think of something else to say, something profound or helpful, but nothing. Instead, all I can hear is Ezra asking if her soul was saved. *It can be saved for a fee.*

"It's all right," he says. "Her memory lives on in a place like this." He carefully lays his palms flat on the table. "I don't want to be invasive, but are you all right?"

My heart does something close to a car colliding at a hundred miles per hour with a wall. "Yes, I'm fine."

"Okay," he says slowly. "You just seemed lost before." I focus on keeping my gaze leveled with his, summoning all the strength I've had to gain through the years as Ezra's daughter. Finally, he nods and repeats, "Okay."

My relieved sigh is hidden by Tonnie as she sets down our plates. I lean in, almost breathing in the food. "I've never smelled anything so wonderful," I whisper, more to the food than Tonnie or John. Michelle's tried to cook for a few church outings, but it's always half-done, burnt, or just plain wrong, so most of her "home-cooked" food is store-bought.

"Well, it tastes even better, right, John?" she asks, hitting John on the shoulder.

John rolls his eyes. "Even if I didn't feel required to say yes, the answer would be yes. I'm already ready for seconds."

LIZ ASHLEE

CHAPTER 3

John

"So, are you going to tell me what all that was about?" Tonnie asks with a gleam in her eye as she slides into the booth across from me, apparently on her break.

"I'm not following," I lie.

"Oh, hell, *of course* you follow. You know *exactly* what I'm talking about."

When I still don't answer, she crosses her arms and gives an impatient huff.

"John Smith," she says. "You and I both know that you don't bring girls around anymore. That was out of the ordinary.

"What? No, it wasn't. I'm friendly." I turn my attention back to my stack of papers and laptop, even though I've lost all my concentration. I went and grabbed my backpack so I could get back to my research. I might have left the house without all of this, but I always had the intention to go back and get them after Kinley left.

Kinley: the subject of my *obvious* weird behavior, despite what I'm trying to lead Tonnie to believe.

"You are very friendly, but you haven't been out on a

date since …" She trails off, obviously trying to remember.

"Since Katie Marceline, who ran fleeing when she saw my closet full of files on Ezra Abel," I finish for her, because why not humiliate myself before she can?

"That's very specific, but yes."

"Well, lunch with Kinley was not a date."

"You're right. Sometimes you just *happen* to eat lunch together with a girl who *happens* to be pretty that you *happen* to be attracted to."

"Geez, Tonnie, I just met her today," I mutter, raking my hand over my face. As much as Tonnie drives me crazy sometimes, I can't help loving her. She's loud and overly honest, but she's all I've got. Accepting her is easy if it means keeping her in my life.

"You asked her for her number, right?"

"Sure," I say, even though the answer is *no*. I wanted to, but she was shy. I got the impression it would be easy to scare her off.

Tonnie is right; Kinley is very pretty. Pretty in a way that made my throat a little dry when I first started talking to her. She had these green eyes that reminded me of the color of trees just before a thunderstorm, long blonde hair that curled against a round face, a scar that made her look unique. Original. Her smile felt like a gift—something to be treasured. But it was also … sad.

That's why I approached her in the first place. I'm fully aware of the fact that I'm drawn to broken people and things. Ever since my dad died, I've wanted to put some good back into the world. It started with mowing elderly peoples' yards. Then volunteering at an animal shelter, where I picked up my loving, albeit weird, dog. I also emceed events helping adults with disabilities and illness for free. Somehow those natural volunteering activities turned into sitting in on every Ezra Abel service and listening, writing, promising myself no one else will be broken in the same way my family was.

I want to help the people who Ezra fools into

following him.

"So, how did the service go on Sunday?" Tonnie asks, slipping from doting aunt/grandmother figure and into someone serious. Even if she doesn't actively pursue her anger, I know it's there. She wants to topple the Church of Life just as much as I do.

I push my laptop forward and lean back in my seat. "The same as usual. He's been doing the healings and the unorthodox preaching, but none of it is up to par with how it's been."

"But you know why that's happening, don't you?" she asks.

This part isn't going to go over very well. I cross my arms, hoping it'll make me look more like a boulder or something indestructible. Tonnie's mostly rabbit in personality, but she can also be rabid when necessary.

"He's onto me," I admit. "I don't believe he realizes who I am. I was too young for him to recognize me, and he's met way too many people to make the connection to Dad. But he can still tell I'm looking for trouble."

"What makes you think that?"

I try to keep the next part nonchalant. "He sent a guy in a uniform after me. I was in the alley, about to go on my run. Next thing I know there's a fist in my gut and a guy threatening me to stop going to the church."

Tonnie leans in, eyes wide. "You should've told me, John. I *need* to know these things."

"I didn't want to worry you."

"Hey," she says, pointing her finger at me. "You're all I've got. You don't get to pick and choose what I worry about."

I'm equally ashamed and guilty. "You're all I've got, too."

"We don't keep secrets from each other, John." She rubs at her temples. "We can't go to the cops, obviously. Well, not until we have irrefutable evidence against him."

"But even then ..." I trail off.

"Even then Ezra Abel has enough clout around here to make that disappear, too."

"We barely have anything to use against him, so we've just got to keep digging, and then we'll figure out where to go with the information."

"Okay," Tonnie agrees. The bell dings above the diner door for the first time in several hours, signaling the beginning of the dinner rush. "Just be careful, please."

"I thought I *was* being careful," I tell her. "But I should've known he's smarter than that."

#

Clancy starts barking at the door the second I shove my keys into the lock. Regardless of who you are, she greets everybody as if they're a burglar. Normally when she sees it's me, she automatically backs down, but not before I get a first-hand experience of how scary she is when baring her teeth.

When I adopted her, she seemed meek and non-confrontational, but as soon as I got the black and white bull terrier, she started growling—even when she's happy—and nearly taking your hand off when you give her treats.

"It's me," I say, pushing the door open. She moves backward, still barking. "It's me."

She finally stops and stands so her front paws are on my legs. I scratch her nose, which earns me a grateful growl.

"Time for work," I tell her, groping at the wall for her leash.

While most people are asleep, I'm the personality for WJWJ radio. It's a responsibility I earned solely because I don't require a lot of sleep. I originally interned for the station while I was in college, and when I graduated, they offered me the job. Evidently, my voice and my odd stories were a hit with our late-night audience. In between spurts of classic rock music, I try to do unsolved mystery and criminal segments, leaving out the one that's always been the most important to me.

I always go out of my way to be friendly with people, but I'm one that mostly prefers to be on my own. I prefer to do my work quietly and unnoticed, without any precession. I guess that's why I assumed I wouldn't call attention to myself at Ezra Abel's church meetings. It's also why I choose to do the night shows—I'm all alone in office space until the next person on-air comes in. I usually bring Clancy in for the company, and because she'll hate me for a week if I leave her alone for too long.

I exchange my Ezra-research backpack for my work-messenger bag, then Clancy and I make our way out to my SUV. She knows our routine by heart, pulling on her leash just enough to where I won't scold her. My apartment has designated spots, so she even knows which car to go to. But instead of waiting patiently as usual, she jerks on the leash, pulling me away from the car, and starts barking at something she thinks she sees.

I roll my eyes and say her name, tugging on her leash. A leaf could blow and she'd go wild. But unlike most times I scold her, she doesn't cower away. Instead, she barks louder and more insistent.

"What do you see?" I ask, then look out into the darkness. *I talk way too much to this dog.* There's nothing to be seen except for a few trees separating the parking lot from another row of buildings. "Car, Clancy," I command, ignoring her barks.

This time she listens and jumps into the car. When I'm in the driver's seat, I use the rearview mirror to search the tree line again. I sigh, not surprised that there still isn't anything to see.

"You're making me paranoid." I shake my head and start the car, then pull out of my place. In the backseat, Clancy whines.

One more glance in the mirror and I swear I do see

something. It's too large to be a deer and too small to be a tree's moonlit shadow. But in the space of a blink, it's gone—whatever it was … if there even was something.

CHAPTER 4

Kinley

Per usual, my father invited parishioners to our house for dinner. To uphold the perfect family persona, Ezra, Michelle, and Prudence all eat downstairs at the table with the guests, while I'm sequestered to my bedroom for the evening. Luckily, I was sent away with a full plate of food, "cooked" by Michelle á la restaurant.

We live in a modest white, rectangular farmhouse on a plot of land a few minutes from church. Because Ezra has an open-door policy with the congregants (and their bank accounts). I spend a lot of my time at home alone. Not that I'm bothered by that. It puts more space between me and the Church of Life, which helps me see through Ezra's tactics. That's more challenging than I want to admit. Sometimes I feel like I'm under his spell—following him as everybody else does.

If I've learned anything, it's that it's easier to follow his commands.

That doesn't stop the pit in my stomach from rearing its ugly head. When I went to the library today in hopes of finding out more about John Smith, I was almost glad when nothing came up about him. But I also realize Ezra will get impatient if I don't find anything soon, which means he'll start exploring other solutions.

"If I could just figure out what you're up to, John Smith," I say, shuffling around my papers as if that will help. It won't.

I spent the afternoon in the library with a very patient librarian who helped me locate all of the articles in their database about Velma and Tonnie. I knew they would be the easiest starting point given I had their full names thanks to the Velma's Vittles website—Velma and Tonnie Rheed. Only two articles mentioned a John Smith. Not my John, though—his father. One was a wedding announcement mostly spotlighting Velma. The other was an obituary:

John Smith, Sr., 53, died on Thursday, Sept. 15th, at St. Agatha Hospital's Hospice Center. He is survived by wife, Emily Smith, and son, John Smith, Jr., as well as his stepmother, Velma Rheed. He will be laid to rest on Saturday, Sept. 17th, at 2:00 p.m. at Weston & Clerks Funeral Home. In lieu of flowers, please send donations to the ALS Association.

With that information, I might be able to find somebody who knows something about my John. Maybe he's attending the church to find peace? Or maybe he's hoping to find a community? Maybe other people who've lost other loved ones?

I chew absently on the breadstick that came with the meal Michelle ordered. What are my next steps? I could look deeper into John Smith, Sr., but that might just lead me somewhere that isn't helpful …

No, I think I'll just have to push my luck with another chance meeting with John. The best way to learn about him is to talk to him.

Ezra barraged me with questions yesterday, and I told him what little I'd learned, which was enough to make him happy. It was hard enough telling him those things, so I can't imagine how it'll be when I know more.

My door suddenly opens and my heart stutters, for fear it's a guest. When someone did accidentally stumble into my room once after one too many drinks, my dad explained away the problem by saying I was a high-profile person's daughter who needed to be healed.

Thankfully, it's only Michelle. She has a glass of wine in her hand, looking more dazed than usual. She closes the door quietly behind her then just stands there. She stares at the rug on my floor, face completely relaxed as though she's not troubled by anything. I've thought more than once about breaking into her stash and trying something—anything—to make me care less than I do.

"Michelle?" I say, resting my arms on my thighs.

"Yes?" she asks slowly, turning her head to look at me. In her world, it's perfectly normal for her to just go along existing and not really noticing—or maybe she's ignoring, I'm not sure which. She used to be a nice person. She went along with Ezra and his illicit activities, but she'd also make sure Prudence and I were comfortable. She was even the one who put forward the offer to adopt Prudence, not realizing Ezra would use her as a bargaining chip. Then, gradually, she turned into this person. She doesn't even talk anymore unless it's to Ezra or a congregant.

"You're in my room," I tell her.

"Yes," she agrees.

"Shouldn't you be downstairs?" I ask.

She looks at the ground, as if Ezra's right below her feet. She's wearing a pair of weathered loafers because Ezra believes "dressing like the common" man makes us more approachable. Meaning, people are more willing to donate to someone who doesn't appear to be profiting from the cause. It makes sense, in a roundabout, crooked way.

"My job's done," she says simply.

I don't exactly know what happens at dinners, but I'm

sure they're as well-oiled as his services. Ezra is always on a mission to complete an objective.

"Is everything okay?"

She holds up her wine. "Yes."

Next time I have to talk to John, I'm going to remember this conversation. Nothing is ever going to be as difficult as trying to talk to Michelle.

"Well, I should probably get back to my research."

"On that man?"

I nod.

"John," she says.

"How do you know that?"

Her shoulders raise slightly. She takes a sip of her wine and turns back to my door. "You should watch Prudence," she says before she slips back outside.

I stare at the closed door, wondering if she was ever really in here to begin with. I'm more likely to believe it was all just my imagination.

#

"You'll need to disappear for the day," Ezra says to me as soon as I walk down the steps a few mornings later. The room is pristine, per usual, with nothing but the necessities on the cream-colored counters. The walls and floors are white, meant to seem minimalistic and older, even though Ezra had them installed new a few years ago. The table in the middle of the room is where we usually eat breakfast. There is always a bounty of flowers in the center of the table. Parishioners send them to us on a regular basis.

His gaze is focused on his laptop, a coffee mug perched at his lips. The Church of Life newsletter is on the screen, with his face front and center as he lays a hand on a newborn's forehead. One of his most loyal parishioners writes the articles for him, but Ezra always has the final say. He's been known to rewrite the entire thing. The articles usually range from doctor testimonials praising

Ezra's healings, accounts of how much the church is donating to the community, and why Ezra's belief in people is more important than his preaching.

In all honesty, the doctors' testimonials are false. But Ezra does do good in the neighborhood. Granted, he's stolen from the church's funds, but he's to the point where he doesn't need the money anymore, so he does put some back into the community. There's this gray line where it is hard to tell if he's doing this for himself or for others. For example, how last week he took personal time to visit one of the dying congregants when there was nothing in it for him. She didn't have money to will him, and if she asked, he couldn't begin to pretend to heal her. It would be obvious it was all fake. He just wanted to make sure she wasn't lonely in her final moments.

But with every good thing he does, there's a bad thing to cancel it out.

"Okay," I say back to him. This isn't the first time he's asked me to leave the house and it won't be the last. I should be insulted that he does this, but I'm actually fond of it. It's a day off —something I don't get often.

"A perspective family is coming by and the kids always end up going places they shouldn't," Prudence says from the seat adjacent to him. She's marking up the agenda for the Church Advisory Board Meeting that meets bi-weekly. Ezra gave her control of it, but he micromanages that, too.

Michelle is standing at the counter, drinking from her own coffee mug. She doesn't look at me, and I can't help wondering if she remembers coming into my room and telling me not to trust my sister.

"Prudence, your father doesn't want you to speak unless spoken to," she reminds Prudence in a faraway practiced tone.

Ezra ignores them both and looks up at me. "Update me on the reporter situation." His gaze flicks over the plain, round clock on the wall. "Quickly."

I swallow, then pour over a quick account of what I've

learned. I try not to look at Prudence, because I don't want to see her expression. She wants me to fail, and here I am, giving her exactly that.

When I'm finished, he lets out a long breath through his nostrils. "That isn't enough, Kinley."

"No," I say. "I'm sorry. I only need a few more days."

"It's already been that long. If you were Prudence, the job would have been finished."

I'm sure Prudence takes it as a win, but I think deep down Ezra knows I was right about John not trusting Prudence.

"I'm meeting him today," I lie. "At his aunt's diner again."

He nods stiffly. "Seeing as we're all indisposed today, I'll give you one more day to find something substantial, or else we're going to find a different approach."

"Thank you," I say, then rush past all of them, keeping my head down, face hidden behind my hair. I don't want him to look too closely at me and change his mind. He might realize that I have absolutely no plans to meet John again, because I'm not sure how to accomplish it. It's not like I can just show up at the diner again.

No, it has to be happenstance.

I quickly put on my gray peacoat, scarf, and gloves, then head outside into the cold. There's a bus stop several blocks away from the church that I usually take because I don't have a car. I cut through our backyard, since I'm not sure when the family is coming by. Ezra would be furious if they caught me.

I check my phone when I get to the stop, realizing I just missed the seven o'clock bus.

I fall down on the bench, ducking deeper into my scarf.

How am I going to do this? My mind has been swirling ever since that first visit, wondering how I can move forward. I'm just not used to interacting with people, let alone initiating the interactions. Plus, I'm a horrible liar. I don't have a lot of practice. Sure, I've watched Ezra be completely false in his talks, but in person he's completely honest. And he expects us to be completely honest in return. I haven't had to tell a lie since those days on the streets ...

"Kinley?"

I nearly jump out of my skin at the sound of John's voice. Like that endless reel of thoughts, I've also heard his voice a hundred times, thinking if I could conjure him in my mind I'd understand him.

"John?" I say, standing up from the bench to see him walking across the street with an Oreo-colored dog on an orange leash. The dog's tail is wagging happily, although there's a certain weariness to its eyes. John is dressed in a black coat and jeans, with his hair messed up and his eyes exhausted. He has a Styrofoam cup in his hand, steam rising up. "What are you doing here?"

He tilts his head, his face contorting as he thinks. After a minute, he comes to a stop in front of me and rubs the hand holding the leash over his face. "I'm too tired to make something up," he says, chuckling slightly. He points vaguely. "I, uh, walk by that church—the Church of Life—every day."

I purposefully keep my expression flat. "Do you go there?"

"Ah, not exactly. What are you doing here?"

No, please don't change the subject. "I live in town."

"Huh," he says. Thankfully, he doesn't seem to suspect anything. In fact, he just smiles at me. "Well, I can't say I'm not happy to see you again."

"Really?" I ask, blushing.

"Yeah," he says as if it's an obvious thing. I wish he'd say why it's obvious because I can't fathom why. "Plus, Tonnie would be thrilled I ran into you again. She's a hopeful believer in star crossing or something. She tends to talk more than I actually listen."

His dog, obviously over the conversation, puts its front paws up on the bench, trying to stand to my height.

"She's friendly, most of the time," he tells me.

I let her sniff my hand, then pet her. She immediately lowers her head, forcing me to pet the bridge of her nose. "What's her name?"

"Clancy."

"Hi, Clancy," I say, leaning in close. "I'm Kinley."

John laughs when Clancy pushes her cold, wet nose into my hand, and I jump. "Do you have dogs of your own?" he asks.

I shake my head. "Al—my mom is allergic. There used to be some that we sort of shared with our neighbors. They would come over every morning and my sister and I would feed them. But that was when we were little."

"That's a shame," he tells me. "I can't imagine not having a dog in my life. Clancy here's been the best of them all, even if she has twenty different personalities." He looks over his shoulder, in the direction the bus will be coming from, then down in the direction where there are a few cars parked at the curb. "Did you have plans for the day, or would you want to spend the day with me and Clancy, here? I make the best breakfast—well, other than Tonnie. But I did learn from her, so I'm pretty accountable."

"No, I didn't have any plans."

"You were just going to hop on the bus and go?" he asks. My heart works in double time, worrying he's actually questioning me, but then he takes a sip of his coffee and grins. "I like it. Spontaneity. So, what do you say?"

I don't know why, but the words that come out of my mouth are, "But you look a little tired?" In my imagination, I can see Prudence rolling her eyes while the vein in Ezra's neck bulges with stress. You were supposed to say yes.

"I'm always tired," he says. "I work best when I'm at ten-percent battery life. So I guess that's a no?"

"It's a yes," I tell him.

John's excitable, proud grin makes it seem as though

I've accomplished something great, even though all I did was accept his offer. Clearly it was the right choice and the choice he wanted. I've never had anyone be so interested in just spending time with me. Normally, if I'm not just being ignored, people are too busy noticing the burn on my face. But I don't think John wants to ignore me, and he hasn't even looked at my burn.

He's not the villain Ezra thinks he is, which I suspected all along. What makes everything harder, though, is I want to know John for real. Not because of Ezra's task, but because he's the first person I've ever met who I feel connected to.

CHAPTER 5

John

Somehow, Clancy winds up on Kinley's lap during the drive back to my place. She's usually sequestered to the backseat, but we're going slow through town and there's no traffic.

Half the time I'm not even sure if Clancy likes me or if she just puts up with me because I'm her owner, but she's taking straight to Kinley. Normally Clancy is wary of any and all strangers, but she acted as if she's known Kinley for forever.

I hope that's a testament to who Kinley is as a person.

Tonnie was right when she said I don't spend a lot of time with people anymore. I've always been a social guy, but it's gotten hard to get close to people over the years. Ever since my dad passed—it's like I see people differently. Everybody I meet appears to me as a potential threat. I used to trust people initially, but now I reward people with trust. I never take anyone at face value, because you never know what's really in their hearts.

I guess that's what I like about Kinley. She might not say much, but everything's in her face. When she's excited or nervous, it's right there for me to read. Even when she's holding back from me or maybe telling a white lie, I can see it. I know there's something beneath the surface—a backstory I don't know yet—but she doesn't read like a liar or someone mean.

She's just *kind* and *open.*

"I apologize ahead of time, my place is sort of a wreck," I tell her.

That seems to make her happy because she hugs Clancy tight and smiles. Then again, maybe it's Clancy that makes her happy. "That just means you have other things to worry about than appearance."

Other than the story about the neighbor dogs, this is the longest sentence she's spoken. I can't help noticing she's not bothering to hide her scar with her hair anymore. Up until now I haven't been able to see the full extent of her burn. It encompasses here entire cheek, eventually disappearing down into her coat. It's clearly an old scar, with no chance of further healing.

Somehow, it makes her seem more of a mystery but also sweeter. The fact that she worries about it—when it doesn't detract from her prettiness—shows she needs a whole lot more love and support than she's been receiving.

This reminds me of a test—as if she wants to see if it bothers me. So, when the light we're at changes green, I remove my gaze and keep it carefully trained on the main road into town.

"You might say that," I agree with her. "Cleaning is definitely the last thing I usually think about, but right about now, I wish I cared more."

"I'm sure it's fine. What keeps you so busy?"

My throat dries as I consider telling the truth or a fabrication of the truth. Tonnie would tell me to fabricate the truth, because it would scare Kinley away, as it has other girls. One of their voices has been echoing in my mind for days, ever since I met Kinley—*You're too obsessed with this man to care about anyone else.*

"I work for a radio station at night, then I also have a pet research project on the side. Plus, I enjoy helping Tonnie out where I can," I explain. It's best to tell the truth, but not the whole truth. For now, at least.

She looks down at my SUV's radio station, which is currently tuned to WJWJ. "Like a real radio station?" she asks, pointing.

"Yeah, this one, actually. I'm their after-midnight personality, although I try to let the music entertain the listeners rather than my personality."

"Wow," she says. "I don't listen to the radio a lot, but now I'll have to."

"You'd have to stay up pretty late."

"Which I usually don't," she says, making a face.

"You can listen to them on the WJWJ website the day after my segments. All of our shows are recorded and uploaded there."

"I'll have to do that. How did you get into radio?"

"Well, I had a specific interest in print journalism, but I got an internship with the station during my junior year and I loved it. I just sort of stayed." I pull into the parking lot behind my apartment. Mostly everybody else is gone for the day. "What about you? What do you do?"

She pulls away from Clancy to fiddle with her scarf. *Deflection.* "I do lighting for a theatre."

"Are you embarrassed about that or something?"

"No," she says slowly. "I just wish I had something else to do."

"Why don't you go find something else, then?"

"Because I can't."

"You sound pretty definitive about that."

Instead of answering, she leans forward to look up at my apartment building. We're on the other side of the building from where we met, no storefronts to be seen. "Is this you?"

"It is," I say. "Mess and all." She laughs and we get out of my SUV, bringing Clancy with her. "You sure you're

41

okay being alone in my apartment with me?"

Her pretty, thin eyebrows furrow. "Why wouldn't I be?"

"To begin with, we're strangers. And that's the second time I've happened upon you." I take Clancy's leash from her, then run my hand over my head. "I didn't realize it was a little creepy until now."

"No, no, not creepy," she manages, giving me a timid glance. I was definitely creepy.

"I can see right through your lies, Kinley," I say.

Is it just my imagination, or did she lose some color?

"You can?"

"You're pretty transparent," I tell her.

She doesn't answer until I've unlocked the outside door and we're heading up toward my apartment. Halfway up the stairs, I let Clancy go free. She's always too focused on getting back home to run away.

"I don't mean to be," she says.

I shrug. "That doesn't mean I know all of your secrets, of course."

She lets out an audible sigh. "Thank goodness."

Clancy paws at my door, then when I open it, she barrels inside.

Normally I don't notice the fact that my place is pretty lived in, but right now I can't help it. I have books on every subject and genre laying around the room, some open, some bookmarked, but most already read with post-its inside to mark the parts I appreciate but will probably never return to. My counters, lounge chairs, and tables are all stacked high, with only one empty spot at the kitchen table and on the sofa. My kitchen is fairly clean, although it's got all the knickknacks from Velma's thrown all over the place. Whatever Tonnie doesn't put in the diner, she usually puts in her house or finds a home for it in my apartment. I get no say, whatsoever.

My desk, thankfully, doesn't seem as conspiracy-theorist-like as I sometimes think it is. Other than a corkboard, my files are all neatly tucked away in a filing cabinet. Ever since Ezra sent one of his goonies after me, I've tried to be more confidential. I bought that cabinet and made sure it had a lock because I wouldn't put it past Ezra to break in here to find out what I have. Ruin it all.

"So, what kind of breakfast can I treat you to?" I ask, trying to shake away my Ezra fog.

"Whatever your specialty is," she says.

"An omelet it is," I say, heading into my kitchen. I motion toward the island. "Have a seat."

She sits, glancing around curiously. I busy myself by getting out everything I'll need, trying not to clank the pans too much, or else it'll send Clancy into hysterics. Really, all I want to do is watch Kinley. Not in a creepy way—or at least I hope not. I guess I'm just an observer, and she's the most interesting study I've ever come across. From the second I saw her the other day, I felt drawn to know more about her. Tonnie could be right about me liking to fix people and things, but it feels like more than that. There's something about this girl I want to unravel and re-ravel myself in.

"I've never seen so many ... things," she says, almost with a sense of awe.

I look over my shoulder at her. "You sound like *The Little Mermaid* or something."

Her brows furrow. "What?"

"Arielle and that Prince something-or-other? She gets legs? 'Kiss the girl?' Disney?"

She only stares at me, her eyes sparkling with laughter at my confusion. How does she not know about a Disney film? God, they've all been written and re-written for every medium you can think of.

"Sorry," she says. "I've never heard of it."

I shrug and start whisking my eggs. "Eh, I was more of a *Power Rangers* guy anyway. To each his own."

"To each his own," she repeats. She's quiet during the time it takes me to make up the eggs and put bread in the toaster. "Hey, John?"

"Yeah?"

"You're very kind," she tells me.

No idea how to answer that. "Uh, thanks, I think."

#

As it turns out, Kinley doesn't know much about anything modern. Hell, she barely even knows about the classics.

I find this out after we've eaten our breakfast and I've turned her loose on my bookshelf. She glanced at it a lot while we were eating, so I figured she was interested. I tried asking her about the authors she enjoys reading, but she couldn't think of any, so I offered up a few of my favorites. All of the authors and titles were clearly new to her.

After that, I tried classics. Really, the only name she recognized was good ol' William Shakespeare.

"I was homeschooled," she explains weakly.

"Yeah, but you read in homeschool, right?"

"Yes," she says with a nervous laugh. "I was in foster care until I was eight, so I was always a little behind in reading. But my adoptive parents were a little ... religious ... so we read the bible, mostly."

"Wow, I'm sorry you didn't get the opportunity to read more," I say, searching the shelf for a particular book. When I find *The Giver,* I hand it to her. "Guess you'll need to get started now, then?"

She takes it from me, flipping through the pages slowly, as though it'll disintegrate. "Thank you."

"Don't thank me until you've read it," I say. "I hope you get the irony in it."

"What's irony?"

"Well, it's a book about pushing past the norm but also about experiencing new experiences. A whole new world, so to speak, which is also a reference to *The Little*

Mermaid."

She smiles at me. "I think you're a little strange."

"I might say the same about you," I tell her. As she flips through the pages, I can't help myself from asking. "I know you said your parents are religious. Do you go to that Church of Life?"

Her hands still and she shuts the book. "No," she says, but fumbles with the book and it falls just in front of her feet.

We both lean down to pick it up at the same time, our faces separated by a slice of air.

It might just be my mind messing with me, but I swear her breath catches. Then again, it might be mine that does. She smells like the first snow of the season—crisp, almost cleansed. Her long blonde hair is barely tickling my fingers, but I can already feel that it's as thick and soft as velvet.

Her gaze dances up to mine, her eyes shimmering in a way that reminds me of lights on a Christmas tree. "Nobody's ever given me anything before," she says quietly.

The urge to lean in closer is almost painful. "I think people should be giving you everything possible."

Her eyes widen, and she falls back on her heels, then straightens. It's so sudden, I stay where I am, bent. She shakes her head, raking her hand through her hair. "I'm sorry, I need to go." The book is clutched in her hand, something I probably wouldn't have noticed if her hands weren't shaking and her knuckles weren't white.

Clancy, who'd been following Kinley as though she's her new best friend, starts barking and spinning in circles.

Hand on the doorknob, Kinley glances over her shoulder, *sorry* on her lips and in her expression again, before she leaves. I'm too stunned, but I can tell by her footsteps she's *running.*

What just happened?

CHAPTER 6

Kinley

"I can't do this, I can't do this," I chant as I walk out into the cold, heading in the opposite direction of John's apartment. There's a bus stop near him, but I have to get away.

I don't know how or why everything went wrong, but it did. His hand touched my hair and he smelled like fire and there was heat radiating from him and ... I thought he could really see *me*.

God, I thought I saw me.

But it was only the me I wanted him to see.

He doesn't know anything other than what I've let him see and what I've told him. If he knew who I really was, I'm sure he'd be revolted. Not just because Ezra is my legal father, but because I've stood by while Ezra's played his little game of psychological warfare.

Even if I knew how to put a stop to him, I'm not sure I would. He's all I have—he's all Prudence has. I have to put Prudence first before I think about the collective. It might not be the right thing, but it's the best I can do.

"Kinley, hey, what's wrong?" John's too much of a

good guy to just let me leave. He huffs out the last words as he jogs up next to me, not wearing a coat, with only one of his shoelaces tied.

I can't look at him or face him, so I keep walking. "I just have to go home."

"Okay, yeah, that's fine," he says. I'm so focused on the sidewalk ahead of us, the only evidence I have that he's still following me are his footsteps and his breath hanging in the air. "I worried there was somethin' wrong, and I don't—it's not right to let people leave like that. Most of the time, that's when trouble strikes."

I stop and turn toward him, still not meeting his gaze. "I didn't mean to just run off."

"I know."

I pull my hair over my shoulder, running my hand over it to flatten it. Between the wind and my nervous hands, it's a mess. "I'm not used to …" I trail off, motioning aimlessly between the two of us. He could take that in a number of ways, and it'd all be correct. I don't know how to deal with men, let alone people.

"That's fine," he says. His face is kind—not the least bit judgmental. "I'm not used to it, either. Honestly, I work too much, and it doesn't leave a lot of room for a personal life." He leans in slightly, making my head fuzzy. "New territory isn't always a bad thing."

"I hope not," I say, offering him a shaky smile.

He crosses his arms, skin pale and prickled from the cold. "Do you need me to drive you somewhere?"

"No, I'll take the bus."

"All right," he says. "But how about I get your number and you text me when you get home?"

I blink. "My number?" I repeat.

A slow smile parts his lips. "Yes, your number."

I'm still dumbfounded.

"Do I need to put it bluntly?" He chuckles and shakes his head. "I honestly care about your safety, but I'm also using it is as a strategy to keep in touch with you."

"Oh," I murmur. I squint. "Really?"

"Just give me your number," he commands, taking his phone out of his pocket.

I tell him my number, and when I finish, my phone immediately dings with a message. I pull it from my pocket and read it: "Hey, it's John."

Just a simple, three-worded text. Nothing more. But my heart soars as if he'd written me a poem and read it aloud in front of an entire room of people.

"I got it," I say quietly. I have to fight the urge not to save the message forever or to make him a favorite contact right then and there. "I'll text you when I get home."

"And we'll talk and see each other again," he adds. "Soon."

Once again, I repeat his final word, both numbly and dumbly. I have nothing left in me but awe and surprise. Those feelings do not leave me—even as I take the bus trip home and then the covert walk back home. When I get there, I pause to send John a text. **Me:** I made it home.

John: Good. I enjoyed being with you today. Let's do it again. Soon.

#

Prudence, Michelle, and I all sit in my special effects room, while Ezra stands before us with a binder open like a bible. This is a several-times-a-week-routine because, despite all of Ezra's flaws, he is a very organized man. To anyone else, he might seem as if he's working off the cuff, but his routine is perfectly planned. He can't stand it when cracks show.

"We are using a plant this week, since the last few weeks have all been real cases. We need something more dire to maintain the congregation's attention. I'm using an actor from a few towns over in exchange for some face time with Mr. Charles." Ezra prefers to use the powerful people in the church to get his bidding done. Mr. Charles is a retired television executive, which means Ezra has a lot of opportunities for young actors to break into the business. Mr. Charles probably knows about Ezra, but he's also synonymous with scandal, so he's been using the Church of Life's good deeds to elevate his standing. "Prudence, you'll take the plant back, put the chicken liver on the napkin. I'm going to say he had brain cancer, so remind him of that."

Prudence's disgust shows for only a split second. "Yes, Daddy." Michelle used to do that, but Ezra thinks she takes too long to get things done now.

"After that, I will remind congregants to meet us at Marla Grayson's insurance company to protest their denying her entry to the diabetes trial. Michelle, did you send in the tip to the news crew?"

Michelle blinks a few times, then straightens. "Yes, dear."

"Good. Kinley, you'll call the news during the protest. More coverage, more parishioners." He flips his page, nodding. "We'll end with donations for the shelter. I want to emphasize how people didn't give as much as they could've last time, which should end in people encouraging each other to donate more. This time, we'll split it forty-sixty between our account and the church's." He closes his book and massages his temple. "Should we expect John to be there?"

"I'm not sure," I reply, holding my phone tighter in my hand. We've been texting sporadically since breakfast. Well, I should say he's been texting me regularly and I've been the sporadic one. I see his texts, but it takes me a while to figure out how I want to respond. I'm using caution to fight off my nerves. It started with me telling him I made it home, which moved into me thanking him for breakfast, which started a conversation about breakfast foods and Tonnie and my favorite foods. It was all simple and easy—him getting to know me and me getting to know him—and *not* what Ezra wants.

Ezra shakes his head, face reddening. "Are you even *trying* to do what I asked?"

"I am," I say, emotions coiling up in my throat. Panic, resentment, misery.

"It doesn't seem like it. It's been a week and he is *still* a problem."

"I'm sorry," I tell him. "It's just taking time."

"I don't remember telling you to take your time," he spits back.

I didn't say *I'm* taking my time, I said *it's* taking time. "I'll try harder," I tell him. "I apologize for being slow."

"Have you at least learned anything that's useful?"

I wish I had something—anything—to make him happy, but that's virtually impossible. Instead, I tell him the most useful thing I know. "He's not a reporter. He does an early morning show for a radio station."

"So he has an audience to speak to," he says, face lined with worry. I think this is the first time he actually looks fifty-something. Whether it is God or good genes, he normally looks younger than his age and more vital. Now, he looks haggard. "An audience who will listen to him. He'll ruin us."

"I'm not sure it's that type of radio station," I explain.

"A reporter is a reporter, Kinley. Don't be naive."

I close my mouth, knowing that no matter what I say, he won't be happy.

"Prudence, you should step in," he declares.

Prudence grins, looking prettier and shinier than ever. It's almost as if she knew he was going to say that because she's wearing her prettiest sweater dress, with her hair curled and more makeup than usual. She sings, "Thank you for the opportunity," just as I whisper, "No."

But I'm not heard, because the three of them are already walking away, Prudence talking about her plans to flip John's loyalty.

#

At first, I don't think John is coming to the service. Maybe it's just hope against all odds or the fact that he's late or that when I ask him his plans for the day he says, *I'm taking Clancy on a hike.* Deep down, I know he was lying for whatever reason he has to lie. I am, too, because I told him I'm doing the effects for a play today.

But then I spot him walking in and taking a seat toward the back. Today he's wearing a knit cap and a pea-coat, almost as if he's trying to hide amongst the group. This time he's not carrying a notebook or even a bag. *How is he going to take notes?*

Maybe Prudence's excitement somehow manifested itself and now John is on our side? No, that's impossible. I'm not stupid, I know she or Ezra are not anything other than human. But there's only so many times you can hear someone say something before you start fearing it's true.

I scan for Ezra, lost amongst the crowd as he greets people. Michelle is appearing to listen to a woman who is talking to her, but she obviously isn't. Her eyes close for long periods at a time. She's holding a coffee that she's been refilling and drinking, which I guess she's using as a measure to keep her awake, but I can't see it pairing well with her pills.

My sister, though, clearly notices John the second he walks in. She has a small crowd around her, arms moving animatedly as she talks to some of the most important and influential congregants. But her head keeps turning in the direction of where John is.

My watch tells me it's three minutes until the service, which doesn't leave her any time to work her magic. At least, I hope not. I could be underestimating her.

Please don't fall for her, John.

CHAPTER 7

John

"Excuse me, where do you think you're runnin' to?" the voice of Little Miss Satan asks just as I'm about to leave—all right, flee—following the service. There's an extra twang to her voice than there typically is, which I guess is her version of a siren call. I had a feeling she was up to something, but I was also hoping it was just in my mind. I don't want this girl trying to put any sort of moves on me, given her age and personality.

Today I switched from notes to audio recording the service on my phone—something easier and less noticeable. I only wish I would've kept the thing on for this conversation.

Prudence is grinning when I turn, hands clasped in front of her. I'll admit that she's pretty, yes, but in a way that's the opposite of angelic. As much as she tries to hide it, you can see the love for catastrophe in her eyes. She likes to witness and cause trouble. Little does she know that I'm good at handling trouble—that as much as she thrives on it, I want to end it.

I take my hat off and put it against my chest, trying to

seem earnest. "The service was remarkable, and I was rushing to my bank to withdraw some money to donate to the shelter."

Her smile widens, showing all her teeth. "How generous of you. Here I was thinking you were running off to write a tell-all."

"Well, that too, of course. Ezra's ability to remove a cancer that even a doctor can't should be known to everyone."

"It is his gift from the Lord Jesus."

"And the chicken," I add, winking.

Her eyes flash with fire, though everything else about her screams sugar and cookies and everything sickeningly *sweet*. "I don't know what you're talking about."

"I'm sure you don't," I say. "Which is amazing because I'm sure the smell is horrible."

She moves her hands to her hips. "You are a problem, aren't you?"

"Evidently," I say. "Given your cop friend's visit and all. I'm surprised you think I'm a big enough issue to warrant that response."

"We've faced other challenges. We know how to identify and handle them," she says. Is she really a teenaged girl or a forty-year-old undercover spy? If she didn't fluctuate between drama queen and this, she might actually be intimidating. She stops talking to pat the shoulder of an elderly woman passing by us. Before I know what's happening, she links her arm through mine and starts moving me toward the middle of the church. Most people are either gathering around Ezra or have already left. I don't like the way her fingernails press into my forearm or how she leans in so close that all I can smell is her suffocating perfume. "But most of those challenges bend with enough force. Most have joined the church. So, what can we do to open your heart to God?"

Open my heart to … *God?* Does she hear herself? How can Ezra and his crazy family do this without going up into flames? I'm not sure what comes next after we die, but I sure as hell do not want to piss off the guy with the keys to the pearly gates by using him in vain.

She leans in closer until her chest is pressed up against my side. I get the feeling that Prudence—despite the pure look she tries to pull off—believes sex sells.

Except I don't want to buy from her. But I'm also smart enough to realize active warfare against the church is not going anywhere. I need to play less on the offensive and go on the defensive—play their game. Act just as much as they act.

I put space between us, then cross my arms and stare down at her. I'm not usually this much of a hardass with anyone, but we're playing a game right now. I have to let her think I'm a contender before I let her win.

"A hundred thousand," I say, quoting what Ezra charged to heal my father.

She smirks. "Done."

"In cash."

"Done also," she answers. "Anything else?"

"No," I say. I have no intention of taking the money and backing down. I'll just be quiet and act more loyal.

While I came into this to ruin Ezra, I also had intentions of getting money to everyone who deserves to be repaid. For now, I'll start the twenty thousand Tonnie was able to spare when my mom approached her about faith healing. The rest of the money will go in an anonymous donation to ALS research.

"Should I let my father know you'll still be coming to church?" she asks.

"Yes," I say decisively.

"Good," she hums. "I would be very sad if you didn't."

I'm sure. "Just ask our mutual friend, the policeman, to stay away from me."

She places her palm against my cheek, patting it. Suddenly she's even closer than before. "Oh, John, we've moved on from that already. Keep up."

My eyebrows raise. "You know my name." How the hell did she figure that one out? Probably that deviant cop. I doubt the police station has a full-on genealogy unit, but probably enough access to records to add two and two.

"You're not as under the radar as you think." She laughs and steps away, her heels clacking. "Next time we'll make you a member, and then you're ours and we're yours."

That's ominous, but from what I can tell, harmless. It usually entails signing a membership book, although I'm not sure what doing so does. Maybe I'm agreeing to hand over my life. Or worse. But they don't know who I really am. John Smith, sure, but unidentifiable against the other million John Smiths.

CHAPTER 8

Kinley

My blood feels as if it's going to boil through my skin as I watch Prudence touch John, clearly trying to persuade him to our side. He doesn't look receptive at all ... but I can't help myself. *She's touching him*, and I'm jealous. I don't want her to toy with him, because he deserves better than her. He deserves better than me, no matter how much my heart tells me I like him.

I take my phone out of my pocket, deciding that I can't let him go. I can't let him fall into Ezra's clutches as everyone else does.

ME: Do you want to get dinner at Velma's?

I watch carefully as he immediately takes a step back, reaching into his pocket. My sister's back is to me, but I can wholly imagine her making her pouty face.

JOHN: Sure. What time?

JOHN: I'm off tonight, so it doesn't matter.

ME: Five?

JOHN: Sounds good. I'm glad you want to spend more time together. I thought it was just me.

I grin down at his text, even though I know it's all a

rouse. If he finds out ... if he finds out, I hope he'll know that my only goal has been to protect him and Prudence. He'll have to see that just because Ezra's my adoptive father, doesn't mean I'm fond of him.

Or that I love him.

Down below, Prudence snatches away John's phone, and I go pale. Maybe I'm just imagining it, but she tilts her head back slightly as if she's about to look back and up at me. John reaches for his phone, but Prudence pulls away and begins typing.

I half expect something to show up on my phone from her, but she hands it back and nothing comes through. She just gave him her number, didn't she?

Oh God, Prudence thinks she's in competition with me.

#

My nerves are shot while I wait for John in the same booth we were in the last time at Velma's. I didn't come into this thinking I would be challenging Prudence. I didn't even think I would be making dinner plans with John. This was just supposed to be a research mission, which would evolve into changing John's mind. Now the plan is all fuddled, and I don't even know what I'm doing.

Prudence very perkily announced that she'd gotten John to agree to back down and be a parishioner. She didn't say how or why, but I'm not sure I want to know. Her means of persuasion would probably make me sick. She isn't as lucky as I am to have had a life where lying, stealing, and sex are no synonymous. Ezra was so pleased with her; he didn't even get on her for interrupting him.

John walks in, grinning at me from the other side of the room as he takes off his coat and hangs it on a latch beside the door. Everyone else here kept their coats with them, but I guess when it's your family-owned diner, you make yourself at home. He's wearing a dark green sweater that has giant buttons at his neck and a pair of dark jeans. I'm glad to be wearing my clunky cream sweater and khakis, although my hair is sort of messed up because I didn't have time to style it. I'm not even wearing any makeup. But I feel more comfortable without it because makeup draws more attention to my scar.

"Hey," he says once he's close enough, then slides into the seat across from me. "Sorry I'm late."

"It's fine," I tell him. "I was early."

"Maybe we'll cancel each other out, huh?" He looks toward the kitchen area. "Has Tonnie bombarded you yet?"

I shake my head. "When I walked by her, she said they're busy getting tomorrow's pies ready."

"This place is busier in the mornings and afternoons, so they usually save that for evenings. You'll have to get a slice after dinner. It's the best thing you'll ever eat."

"You're very partial, you know," I say, smiling at him. But my smile fades and I can't look at him as I move toward a new topic. "So, how was your day?"

"It could've been better."

"Oh?" I ask innocently.

"Yeah," he confirms. "I had all these plans and they went south, but I think I figured out how to improve on everything. But now there's other factors—things I really *don't* want to deal with—and I have to add them into the fold. That's not what we're going to talk about though, okay?"

"Are you sure? I don't mind."

"I do," he says, leaning forward on his forearms. "You're too easy to talk to."

"It's because I don't talk much."

"That does leave more room for me, seeing as I am a talker, but I'd say it's more than that."

My heart does a little flutter. I swear, there's a glimmer in his eyes. Maybe I'm imagining it out of hope.

Tonnie walks up, powder and other ingredients

splattered on her apron. "I didn't get a chance to say I'm happy to see you back, Kinley. Especially since it puts such a huge smile on this one's face," she says.

"Ah, Tonnie, don't be embarrassing," John mumbles.

"Don't be a baby," Tonnie says back, waving a hand in dismissal. "What can I get you two?"

"I'll take a burger with fries and a Coke," John answers.

Tonnie nods, not needing to write it down. "I'll take the same, except with a sweet tea," I tell her.

John holds up two fingers. "And we'll take two slices of apple pie."

"Noted," Tonnie tells us and then walks back to the kitchen.

"Transparency is definitely her strong suit," John says.

"I think that's admirable," I tell him. "I wish more people were like that."

"Agreed, even if it is embarrassing as hell."

Quiet settles between us. "I started reading the book you gave me," I blurt, trying to start a conversation for once. I've never been good at just talking.

"Are you liking it?"

I nod, naming a few sections I've enjoyed and ones I'm unsure about. By the time Tonnie comes with our meals, I have a better understanding of what I'm supposed to take away. There's a layer of analysis I didn't realize comes with reading works other than the bible.

"There are sequels," he says, taking a bite of his burger. "But I think maybe I'll give you something else to try next. Maybe *Of Mice and Men* or *Death of a Salesman*."

"I've never heard of either of those."

"There's something exciting about being your reading guide. I can't wait to lend you some of my more recent favorites. You're a blank slate."

"I wish I wasn't," I tell him. "I feel so behind."

"I guess you probably wish your parents would have done things differently, then?"

"More than anything," I admit.

"Do you mind if I ask what happened to your biological parents?"

"No, not at all." I finish chewing my food, then take a long drink of my tea. Talking about my mom and dad is almost too easy. I was too young to have any real memories of them. All I really know about my parents is the information on my record. "I had a dance recital. My parents left my little sister with a babysitter because she was still too fussy to take and they wanted the night to be special and only mine. They took me to dinner afterward, which kept us out later than usual. On our way home, a man in another car fell asleep at the wheel. My dad swerved to miss him and we went off the road instead. My parents died on impact."

"Kinley," he says. His voice saying my name is a comfort I didn't realize I needed. He reaches out, touching his rough fingertips lightly against my hand. Nobody's ever reached for me or held my hand before. Tingles run up my arm and into my head, making me feel lightheaded. "I'm sorry. But that never helps, does it?"

"Coming from you, it does."

"Is that how you got your scar?"

I take my hand from his, immediately hiding my scar.

"No, don't." He sits forward fast, reaching across the table so his large hand is covering my small one. He brushes his thumb over my weathered skin, while he tangles his other fingers in my hair, massaging my scalp. "I think it's beautiful. I think *you* are."

I blush. "Thank you."

"This is where you tell me I'm handsome and dreamy," he says ironically, eyes sparkling. He pulls back, serious again. "You shouldn't be self-conscious of your scar when it's a part of who you are."

"I know," I admit. "It's just hard because it's right there and people notice it. They think it makes me different."

"Kinley, I hate to tell you, but you are different. Except

it's not because of the scar. It's that shine you got to you."

"Shine?"

"I know, it sounds weird. But there's just something so *pure* and *sweet* about you. It feels like a man could purge his soul to you and have it healed. When I first saw you, you looked so lost and I felt pulled to you. I thought it was because I wanted to help you, but I'm beginning to see I might be the one who needs you."

"You don't need me," I tell him, earnestly. *You don't need Ezra's daughter.* The *sweet* and *pure* description seems false and dirty. I wish I could be what he thinks I am.

"I think you'll come to realize I do. There's things I haven't told you because I don't want to scare you off. But I will tell you. Eventually."

Does he mean about Ezra? Or maybe Prudence?

We both go back to eating. As I chew on a fry, I realize I didn't answer his question. I should just let it pass with the rest of the conversation, but I want to tell him as much as I can so the truth can outweigh the lies. "It was a car fire. I was stuck in my car seat until a fireman was able to rescue me."

"That must have been terrifying."

"It was." I might not be able to remember my parents, but I can still remember the smell of my skin burning. How my entire body was cold, while my cheek burned like molten lava. I remember screaming shrilly in pain and then *nothing.* According to the records, I passed out from pain. When they pulled me out, they thought I was dead.

"All I can say is I'm thankin' God you're here with me now," he says.

He's not thanking a false version of God. He's not thanking God that I'm here to swindle money from people. He's thanking God because I'm alive and *here* with him.

For the first time in my life, I feel real religion.

Thank you, also, God.

#

"I can't believe Tonnie was out of ice-cream," John grumbles, genuinely dismayed. "You can't have cherry pie without ice-cream."

He told Tonnie just as much while we were there, then asked her to put the pies in to-go boxes. They were both smiling through the conversation, but pie without ice-cream was clearly a serious crime. To remedy the situation, he brought me back to his place, where I'm sitting on the couch with Clancy next to me, her head on my thigh. John is in his kitchen, scooping ice-cream into the bowls where he also puts the pie.

He points at me with the scooper, rolling his eyes.

"You know, I wouldn't doubt it if Tonnie really did have ice cream."

"Why wouldn't she have given it to you then?"

"Because now we're here and not there. She's always trying to do things like that. How I ever get anything done with her around, I'll never know."

"At least we still get to eat pie?" I offer.

"Right, right, bright side." He puts away his tub of ice-cream then brings me my bowl. He sits down on the couch with me, Clancy between us. "Be careful. Clancy has a thing for pie."

On cue, Clancy looks up at me but doesn't move the rest of her body. She eventually lays her head back down.

"She's a different dog when you're around," he mumbles.

"It's probably because I'm more likable," I say, giving a try at humor.

He rolls his eyes, taking a spoonful. "Eat your pie."

I laugh but do as he says. All I've had is the pie the church ladies bring in as a gift to Ezra, but since they're older, the pies are usually burnt or the wrong ingredients were used. One elderly man makes a chocolate pie, which is good, but sometimes he ruins it with alcohol.

Tonnie's pie, though, tastes like the heaven I've heard preached about. The crust is light and fluffy. The cherries are tart, countered by the vanilla ice-cream.

"This is really good," I say over a mouthful.

"You can say that again," he agrees. "Tonnie's pies are one of the best-kept secrets in the family. They always say it's been passed down from generation to generation. Really, though, it came from some magazine my great-grandma used to read."

"Well, it might be a fib, but at least it's a tasty fib," I tell him.

"Yeah, I suppose there's worse to lie about."

"Will you eventually take over the diner?"

"Probably, but I don't have the heart for it. I've always thought when the time comes, I'll hire someone who has the passion to run it. That way it's still in the family, but I'm doing my own thing."

"What would that be? The radio?"

"Maybe, although the night shift wouldn't be a good deal when I have a family. I'd like to maybe shift to daytime radio, then focus on writing non-fiction. I'm fascinated by that area. Nothing's more crazy than things that happen in real life."

"It's all got to come from somewhere," I agree. He yawns, which reminds me that he's probably been up for forever, between working at the radio station last night then going to church. Although he doesn't know I know about that. "You seem a little tired. Do you want me to go home?"

He shakes head. "No," he says. "Remember, I run best at ten percent."

"Okay, but I'll leave when you want me to."

"Then you might be stuck here for a while," he says with a wolfish grin. He squirms suddenly, reaching for his phone in his pocket. When he takes it out, it's lit up and vibrating. "It's work. I'm going to step into my room. One of the guys struggles with technology and he always calls me instead of an IT guy. I'll be back."

He says the last sentence as if he's being sent off into the Amazon on a grave mission.

He shuts the door behind him and I glance around the room, observing his desk—piled high with documents and books—and a locked filing cabinet beside it. Both things have been bothering me since I got here. I look down at Clancy. "What's the right thing to do here?"

Clancy lets out a long sigh.

Nothing's right. Every move is against somebody's best interest. I'll betray someone no matter what I do. I have to choose between protecting John—whom I've barely known and who *doesn't* know me—and Prudence. John is a new friend with the potential for more, and Prudence is the last living family member I have left. She's the only person I've ever loved. But she's also dark, while John is just a good person.

I move out from under Clancy and walk over to the table, trying to be as quiet as possible. I keep my gaze trained on the door John went through, just in case.

Trying to do a quick peek, I sort through the papers. Most of them are just scribbled notes that pertain to his radio show. The stack of books varies in subject. One immediately catches my eye because it deals with constitutional rights. If he was going to use anything against Ezra, it would have to be the law. Even then Ezra's always been very careful about the way he conducts his business.

I pull it out and run my fingers over the cover, hoping it'll offer some deeper understanding of what this all means. When I open it to the first page, there's a picture of a man who looks exactly like John, except his hair has grey streaks in it and he has a beard. The picture is clearly well-loved, with the back turning a smoky cream and the edges curled.

I carefully flip to another page, which has highlights and notations in the margins.

"What are you doing, Kinley?"

John's voice startles me, making me jump and slam the book shut. His doesn't warrant my reaction, because he doesn't sound angry, just resigned. Guilt is what made me slam it. When I look back at him, his shoulders are slumped and his forehead is furrowed. He looks broken almost.

"I was just looking through your books," I say in a half-truth. The piece of it that is a lie tastes like sand.

"Yeah, I should've thought about that. I usually keep everything ..." He trails off and rubs his hand down his face, no more smiles to be seen. "I didn't want you to see any of that yet."

"Why?" I ask, setting the book down and moving closer. "There's nothing wrong with anything there."

"Yeah, except there is. There's this whole messed up situation, and it's basically me against the world. Most people don't understand it."

"I might," I offer.

He gives me a half-hearted smile. "You might," he agrees. "But even if you do understand, my research ... it runs my life. Ruins it, too."

"I don't understand."

"I know, and I don't know how to explain it, except to tell you everything. You were bound to find out about all of this sooner or later." He motions over his shoulder, toward the couch. "Let's sit back down."

We do, except this time Clancy jumps down and heads toward his bedroom, sensing her father's suddenly tense mood.

John scratches at the back of his neck, searching for words. "You remember how I brought up the Church of Life?"

"Yeah, the church I live near."

"Well, it's turned into this megachurch that everyone seems to go to because of the good deeds it does. There's also this belief that the leader, Ezra, can heal people.

Except … he can't, and the deeds are mostly bad. Everything the church does is corrupt, and I promised myself a long time ago I would do something to stop it all. People don't deserve to be treated like sheep who need to be herded."

I swallow. I wish he wasn't right on every account. "How do you know that? What made you …" I trail off because all of a sudden he gets a faraway look as Michelle sometimes gets, except his isn't from pills.

"My dad had ALS. After a while, there's really nothing you can do. The second you're diagnosed, all you can do is try an experimental treatment or use medicine to numb some of the pain. It all cost more money than insurance was willing to cover. I think we were all desperate to keep him with us. He was desperate to stay, too. When we realized he was reaching the end, my mom came home with this flier from a friend who swore that Ezra from the Church of Life could heal him. We all knew it wouldn't work, but we were too grief-stricken to see through his smoke and mirrors."

He squeezes his hands, closes his eyes. "Ezra charged us a hundred thousand dollars to heal my dad. You know, that's actually not that much compared to the rest of the debt they'd accrued from the medical bills. But Ezra demanded *cash*. My parents borrowed some from Tonnie and Velma, then my mom had to come up with the rest. I don't know how she got it, but she managed somehow. So we paid Ezra and the following Sunday he called my dad up for his healing. Except it didn't work. He *blamed* my dad's lack of faith, as if my dad's condition was his fault. He *humiliated* my dad. More than that, he took advantage of us when we were at our lowest. He stole the rest of our hope, then basically gloated about it. He threw my family out in the middle of the service. After he told us my dad would be going to hell, you'd think he would have offered to help save his soul. But, no.

He opens his eyes and flexes his fingers. "We all gave

up after that. My dad only made it a few more days. My mom … she ended up having a heart attack a few months later, and I can't help but blame Ezra for that, too. He broke all of our hearts, and I can't pretend it didn't wear my mom down into nothing.

"I started collecting as many things about Ezra as I could find, hoping to find something to stop the healings and all of the cruel things the church does. My girlfriend at the time complained to Tonnie about how distant I was, and Tonnie got curious. She's been helping me since then. I've even been going to some of the Sunday services. I just need to find something—*anything*—to end it all."

I don't know how to answer him. It's all so clear now—his grudge against the church and why he's been taking the notes. It's not about an exposé, it's about justice. It's about making sure that what happened to his dad doesn't happen again. I don't remember his dad being healed—there's been so many—but I remember the ones like it. Sometimes, when people are willing to pay, he'll take on the tough cases. Normally, he chooses temporary ailments—headaches, stomach bugs—or he uses the planted parishioners. When we do use the plants, it can be easy to pretend we aren't doing anything wrong. But when they're real people with real problems, you can't ignore the psychological homicide happening. Ezra is their last hope, and then he bludgeons that hope.

"Isn't that enough for the authorities?" I ask, already aware of the answer Ezra orchestrated.

"He has so many people in attendance at his church, there's enough cops to make anything I say disappear. What I've been looking for is hard evidence that's indisputable. Until I have that, I can't expect anything to stick."

"What are you looking for?"

"In a perfect world, I'd catch them in the act of a fake healing—I'd use it against the church to tear them down or at least show its believers the truth. But it would also help to figure out where all the money from the healings is going to. I've just been taking a lot of notes, and I started recording the services. Hoping something sticks."

"And you and Tonnie are doing this all on your own?"

"For now." He looks down at his phone, then holds it up. My sister's name is clearly displayed on the screen as having texted him. *Oh no.* "Plus, today they approached me. Well, Prudence—Ezra's daughter—did. I think she was trying to come onto me and scare me at the same time, but she's honestly just as horrible as her father."

What would he think if he knew I was Ezra's other daughter? "What did she want?"

"She wanted me to stand down. She's a greedy person, so I know she's not going to expect any different of others. So, I asked for a hundred thousand in hush money. I'll pretend to buy into the church if it means I can keep working at this."

"At least you can keep doing what you were doing, just more quietly."

"I guess so," he agrees. "I just wish I didn't have to pretend with Prudence. I mean, she's been texting me and demanding I go to dinner with her. She's not taking no for an answer. And hell, no means no."

Prudence doesn't like that word. Unless it comes from Ezra, it's not in her vocabulary. "Why don't you try lying to her?" Great, now I'm suggesting to lie within a lie.

"I don't think there's much I could tell her to get her off my scent. I mean, I don't think she has boundaries, so who knows what she'll pull. I tried telling her I was seeing someone and she just kept pushing. I should've made leaving me alone one of the terms." He leans forward slightly, catching my hand with his so they're touching as they were in earlier. "I didn't scare you off, did I?

"No, you didn't."

"Really?"

"Not at all. I think—I think I want to help, if I can."

He smiles at me, almost like he doesn't believe me. I

can't help smiling back, but my smile fades into nervousness when he leans in so his face is inches from mine.

"Would you mind if I … can I …"

He trails off, but I answer in a whisper, "Yes."

His lips find mine, pressing softly and sweetly, the perfect pressure to make my entire body feel weightless and my heart beat heavy. I lean in closer, wanting the feeling to envelop me completely. He squeezes my hand, while he uses his free hand to tangle in the hair at the back of my neck, as he deepens the kiss. But before it goes any further, he pulls back, resting his forehead against mine.

My brain is too numb to say anything. My first real kiss. I honestly didn't believe I was worthy of anything so perfect, so kind. But somehow the kiss came true, and it was more than I ever dreamed. More than I wanted.

"This—what's happening between us—feels easy," John murmurs.

It's only easy because I made it easy by setting all of this up. All the good feelings disappear and all that's left is disgust for myself.

John pulls back, lines etched in his forehead. "Sorry, did I do something wrong?" he asks raspily.

"Not at all," I say in a breathless rush, "It's just me. I'm—this is all new."

"But you're not running?"

"No, I'm not," I tell him. "I'm staying."

"Good," he says. "You know, I haven't told anyone about my past in a long time. It means a lot that you listened and tried to understand. Not many people have done that."

"I think most of the time people see what they want to believe, so it's hard to face the truth," I tell him, thinking of myself and all the rest of the congregants.

"You're probably right," he says. He motions toward the TV, then says, "What do you say we watch a movie? Something uplifting?"

"Let's do that," I answer.

"Come here, Kinley," he tells me. I shift toward him and he wraps an arm around my shoulders. I melt into him. As he searches for a movie, I mess with the fabric of his T-shirt.

That kiss changes things.

It marks the point where I went from being able to tell him the truth without any forfeiture, but now … well, now I can lose everything up to and including my heart. If he figures out any of my lies, he won't forgive me. He'll think that I was just using him.

If I'm going to tell him, I need to make the decision soon or face the consequences.

LIZ ASHLEE

CHAPTER 9

John

During the Monday evening quiet period at the diner, I help Tonnie wipe down tables. One of her evening waitresses had to take the evening off last minute, so poor Tonnie's been having to pull double duty. Not that this workload is any different than her normal one. I mean, she takes time to talk to every customer that comes in and is often here from open to close.

We might not be related by blood, but I'll go ahead and say little to no sleep runs in our family. Insomnia is our superpower.

"I swear, I don't know what these people do to these tables, but goodness they're dirty," Tonnie says, scrubbing especially hard at a spot on one of the glass tabletops. "Maybe I need to stop letting people pour their own syrup. If they're going to eat like children, I'll treat them like children."

"You're all talk."

"Say that to that Jesse Adams. Every morning he asks for orange juice, but then only drinks half. What a waste. I told him, if you don't start drinking all of that, I'm only going to give you half. So that's what I've been doing."

"If Jesse Adams is paying for the juice, why do you care if he drinks it or not?"

She stops wiping and looks at me as if I've done gone and lost my mind. "Because it's good for his health," she says. "I don't feed these people every day and learn their life stories just to have them die because they haven't drunken their juice."

"Tonnie, you know juice just builds up an immunity to colds, right? It doesn't keep you from having a stroke or getting cancer?"

Tonnie huffs. "Of course, I'm not dumb. But these things add up, you know? They play into recovery."

All I can do is shake my head, not surprised by Tonnie's stance. If I collect broken people, she collects random people to be fake family members.

"So, how did things go with Kinley last night?" she asks, clearly trying to not act overly curious.

"You're not as subtle as you think," I tell her.

"Sure I am. I could've said, 'Did you kiss her yet?' but I wasn't going to go about it that way."

"Well, color me surprised," I say blandly. "The answer is yes, I did."

She pauses momentarily to look up at me and grin, teeth showing and everything. "Good, *good*." She turns serious and points her dirty towel at me. "Now, don't you ruin it."

"I don't think I will this time." I take a break from my own cleaning and slide into one of the booths. The only person in the restaurant currently has earbuds in; I can hear his music from here. Both of them could care less that we're talking, let alone what we're talking about. "She found some of my research, so I told her."

"What exactly did you tell her? Was it just your general interest in the Church of Life or …"

"Everything—Ezra, the healings, Dad, even Prudence."

"What's that little hellion got to do with anything?"

"She wants me to be her plaything, I think," I admit.

Tonnie turns green. "Lucky you."

"Hopefully she'll get the message I'm not interested, or else I'll probably have to go into hiding."

"As long as that means she doesn't come knocking on my door to find you." She unties her red apron and hangs it on the back of a chair, then walks over to where I'm at. She puts a knee on the padded seat, her hands on her hips. "So she took everything okay."

"Better than okay, honestly. She offered her help."

"I like the girl, but should you have told her so soon?

"Why wouldn't I?" I say slowly.

Tonnie raises an eyebrow. "It's never ended well the other times you've told the women you date. I just don't want to see you get hurt."

"I know, Tonnie. But you've seen how Kinley is. She's different—she cares. I mean, she gets how it feels to lose people you love. She lost her parents. I'm sure she can see how that would be made much worse if someone played into your grief. Besides, you're in this too, so that makes it *our* crazy."

"Yes, well, everyone knows how I am. You're unsuspecting. Well, when you used to talk to people, at least."

"How many times do I have to say that I still talk to people?"

"Clancy doesn't count. But you know what I mean. You're a social guy, but you've turned into a recluse," she says.

"I know, I know. I'm more interested in Ezra Abel than I am in other people. If I could just figure out a way to stop him, I'd have more room in my life."

"Honey," she says, sitting down completely. She reaches out and pats the table, as if it were my hand. I suddenly feel like a kid again. "Have you ever thought about what happens if we can't bring him down?"

"Every day I do, Tonnie. Every damn day." I sigh and

look out the window, at the few stragglers walking around. "But then I think I about how I can't let that be an option. I *have* to put an end to Ezra and the Church of Life."

"I'd be lying if I said I don't feel the same way. But I … your dad wouldn't want you to waste your life on this. Me? I've basically lived mine fruitfully, so I've got space to waste. You? You've got your entire life ahead of you, and I don't want to see you waste it on that church. I know you won't stop, but do me a favor and don't let this opportunity with Kinley pass by. I might not understand her interest, but I do know she's a good girl, and I think she could hold a spot in your future if you let her."

"I hear you, and I agree. I don't think she's one I want to let get away."

"If you feel that way now—after one kiss—you sure as hell shouldn't," she says, chuckling. She slides back out of the booth and heads back to her table. "Okay, time to stop gabbing and get back to work."

"You're the one who started it with your diatribe about orange juice."

"Well, it's important. Make sure you drink it, too."

#

I check my phone one final time, confirming the time Kinley's bus is supposed to get here. I've been sitting at the bus stop for a while, in case she gets here sooner. Since she showed so much interest in the radio show, I invited her to come to the station with me tonight. As it is, I bring my dog, so why not bring Kinley?

Okay, so maybe I'm doing a little more than playing into her interest. I also want to impress her. I don't think you can blame a guy for that. Especially after I told her about—Tonnie's words—my crazy. I think we need a little levity.

I hear the bus's engine before it turns onto the main road, lights illuminating the road. Right on time, despite my anticipation.

The bus stops and it's only Kinley who gets off, wearing a nice pair of teal pants and a black coat. She gives me a shy smile, scrunching her nose. "I wasn't sure if I should dress nice."

I motion to my jeans. "It's just me there. Although I've got to say, I'm very impressed with your professional clothes. You get a checkmark in workplace attire. We'll just have to make sure we measure your efficiency, social skills, strengths, and weaknesses before the night is finished, or else you won't get that end of the year Christmas gift card to a steakhouse."

"Is that really a thing?" she asks. "Do jobs do that?"

"Mine does," I say. "Yours doesn't?"

"No."

"Lucky." I point up to the whereabouts of my apartment, where you can hear Clancy barking faintly. "We have to grab Clancy before we go."

"We're taking Clancy with us?" she asks, clapping her hands.

"It softens the blow of annual reviews," I tell her, winking. *Why the hell did I just wink? That's weird.*

Why am I even concerned about this stuff?

She looks up at me, blushing, and it dawns on me that I'm *crazy* into her—even with barely knowing her—so of course I'm going to be overly self-conscious. Although, I guess if I haven't scared her off by now, I might be in the safe zone.

I walk close to her, eventually summing up the courage to twine my hand with hers. I feel like a middle school kid who's dating a girl for the first time. She bites her lip, grinning. This is one of those moments where it's as if you've won the biggest competition of your life. You're walking on air—pride filling your chest.

When we have Clancy, we head toward my SUV.

"So, do you want to say something while I'm on the radio?" I ask her when we're almost halfway across the parking lot.

"Am I allowed to do that?"

"Well, yeah," I tell her. We come to a stop beside my car and I open the passenger door for her and Clancy. "Might even let you pick a couple of songs."

"Wow, I've never—"

Clancy starts barking, exactly as she did the other night. I look off in the direction she'd been looking in before, but then I realize she and Kinley are both looking at something behind me. Whatever it is, Kinley looks a little panicked.

When I turn, I feel that same panic.

Standing just behind me is *Prudence,* wearing all white— a creepy angel of death. White coat, white pants, white shoes. Her eyes are glimmering in the moonlight, blood-red lips pulled into a smirk.

"John, you didn't text me back," she says, pouting.

Clancy keeps barking beside me, while Kinley clasps her hand on my coat at my back. Her body shrinks into mine.

"Clancy, quiet," I command. "What are you doing here, Prudence? How do you know where I live?"

She smiles. "My family makes it our business to know these things. Although, we didn't know you were *seeing* someone."

Her sharp gaze shifts to Kinley, while Kinley stands up on her toes to whisper in my ear, "John, can we please go?"

I nod. "I have to go to work, Prudence. Can we talk later?" *Or never?*

"No," she says. "I don't particularly like being pushed off, especially by friends. I thought we're friends now, John."

"We are, but friends don't follow friends to their houses. Was that you the other day? Was Clancy barking at you?"

Her smile says yes. "What would ever make you think

that?"

I let out a long breath. Clancy starts barking again, but this time I don't tell her to quiet down. "What do you want?"

She tilts her head. "I *wanted* to get dinner with you at your step-great-whatever aunt's diner, but it looks like you're otherwise engaged with your friend here ..."

I hate the way she looks at Kinley. Prudence reminds me of a vulture, circling an animal until the animal dies. "Like I said, I have to go to work." I try to keep my voice leveled. It didn't bother me when Ezra sent the police officer after me, because I was the one facing the consequences. But it's different when Kinley is here. Different now that Prudence knows Tonnie is my family. I can't even begin to imagine what Prudence or the rest of the Abels are capable of, and I refuse to put Kinley or Tonnie in their line of fire.

"Fine, we'll do dinner tomorrow," Prudence says, leaving no room for argument. There's a challenge in her eyes, but it's aimed toward Kinley. "I'll find you."

She turns, her hips swaying exaggeratedly as she walks away into the darkness. If it were anyone else, I might worry about their safety, but not Prudence.

I motion for Kinley to go ahead and get in the car. Clancy jumps in behind her. As soon as I get in, I lock the doors. "That was Prudence Abel," I explain. "She's not as good at playing me as she thinks she is, but I'll admit she sets my hairs on edge."

"She seemed ..." She trails off, clearly searching for the right word. "Intimidating."

"Pair that with determined and she's one to be reckoned with." I pet Clancy's head before I start the car up, reverse, and drive toward work. "From what I've gathered, she's only seventeen. I don't know why she's trying to use her wiles on me, considering that would mean I've got about eight years on her."

Kinley mumbles something.

"What was that?" I ask.

"She's probably trying to create a backup plan," she says.

"How's that?"

"If you go against the church, they could use a relationship with her against you."

"That's disturbing. I know Ezra sinks low, but would he go as low as sending his underage daughter out to incriminate me?"

"If he's as corrupt as you say he is …"

She trails off, but I can't help seeing her point. I shake my head, unable to make my disgust disappear. "We're lucky because my morals are too strong for that."

"That's what I thought," she says, then puts an arm around Clancy. "I'm sorry about what happened back there."

"*What?* Why should you be sorry?"

"I don't know. I worry I just made things worse. And now you have to have dinner with her tomorrow."

"I don't *have* to do anything," I remind her. "I might have said I'll sign Ezra's Book of the Damned Cult, but that doesn't mean I'll do anything at his daughter's whim. Ulterior motives or not, there's are a million other better ways to prove myself."

"She just didn't seem like the type to give up."

"You're probably right," I agree. "But, you know what? She *is* the type to grovel at the feet of her father. And he's a lot more worried about me than he is of her, so I'll bet if she gets to be a problem, he'll make her back down."

"But I'm sure she still sees you as a threat. What if another way is easier?"

"This isn't the mob. He can't put my body in cement and dump me in the water," I tell her, trying to bring in some humor.

She doesn't bite. "Please don't risk yourself, John. I think you've spent so much time researching Ezra Abel, that you might've forgotten that he's a real person who can do damage."

"Kinley, I know he's real. Trust me."

She sinks into her seat, visibly shrinking away from the conversation. "I shouldn't have put it that way."

"But you did, and I hear you. Just because … just because I'm stubborn doesn't mean you need to get meek on me. Even if I don't want to listen to your opinions, I want to hear them, all right?"

"The same goes for you," she says, reaching out slowly and putting her hand on my knee. She closes the distance between us, Clancy squeezed in the middle.

"I think we might make pretty good partners on this case," I tell her. I like the sound of that—*partners*. I've always had Tonnie, but this feels different. I've finally found someone to share my world with. Maybe even give the world to. Previously, everything felt temporary, waiting for change. But now … I feel still.

#

Kinley chokes every time I try to put her on the radio. Either her face turns redder than a sunburn, she starts stuttering random syllables, or her eyes get all wild as she shakes her head like a bobblehead. Stage fright I guess you could call it.

But we're at the final segment before I slip the listeners into the last half-hour of my show, which I usually make commercial-less. This time, I don't even ask her if she's interested—instead, I turn my mic on and lean in, lowering my voice. My boss said it's more soothing.

"Today, I have a very special co-host here with me. No, not my dog this time. Although Clancy is here. Today, I have a friend in and she's been nervous to say hi. So, without further ado, let me welcome Kinley to the FM. Say hello, Kinley."

Kinley leans in, her cheeks hollow and her eyebrows clear up to her hairline. "Hi," she murmurs.

"Great job," I mouth, which earns me an eye roll that ends in a grin. Out loud, I continue with few advertisements, followed by messages from viewers. I try to commentate on some, especially messages from people who enjoy my show. I also mention a viewer complaint that I play too much old music. I answer, "When you realize 'Africa' isn't by Weezer or 'House of the Rising Sun' isn't from Five Finger Death Punch, then do me a favor and ask that question again. Right, Kinley?"

Kinley blinks, staring at me. "I don't know what you're talking about," she says, then throws her hands over her mouth. "Everybody heard that, didn't they?"

"We are on air. My friends, Kinley, here, is one of my favorite people, currently. She is a blank slate for all things pop culture." I wink at her, hoping to remind her it isn't a bad thing. "I'm jealous of her. Who doesn't wish they could relieve the first time they heard 'Sister Christian' or 'Hey Jude' or 'Bohemian Rhapsody?' They're experiences I wish I would've cherished, but instead I get to cherish Kinley's."

She blushes, and I honestly forget I'm hosting a radio show. All I see, hear, and know is her. I'm lucky, because my phone buzzes, or else I might be three seconds away from losing my job. No matter how much my boss likes me, dead air is not a people pleaser.

I chuckle as I read over the text. Anytime a viewer writes in, it always gets sent to our phones so we can see them during the show in real-time. "Mark J. wants to know if Kinley and I are together, and if not … well, that's a little inappropriate for our family radio show. Mark, we try to keep it PG here, but to tell you the truth, this is all pretty new to us. I can't see what she sees in me."

"I can't see what *you* see in *me,*" Kinley says.

"Well, I can definitely see ratings raising, given how many texts we're getting."

"Am I being used?" she asks, wide-eyed and mocking. She might just have the personality for this show. I figured it was there; she just needed the space to open up.

"Well, Clancy wasn't getting too far since people can't see her. They can hear you, though."

"People can hear Clancy, too, they just can't understand her."

I shake my head, a little mystified by the girl in front of me. Her arms are crossed, she's grinning from ear to ear. It's only been a few days, but I can't help noticing how different she already is. It's like we're both clay, molding ourselves to fit each other's lives.

"You know, I think we might make Kinley a regular. Make sure you write that into the big boss, folks. Unless we want Kinley to be an unpaid, un-hired intern forever. Sadly, I've got to say good-bye and take us into the Morning Rush. We'll start things out with a little Aerosmith."

I switch the audio player on, which already has the music for the next forty-five minutes timed out. I'll just need to supervise it until the host of Morning Rush comes in. Once our mics are muted, I roll my chair closer to Kinley's.

"You've got talent," I tell her. I point toward my phone. "The masses are saying so."

"I'm sure they just like a little change."

"No, they like a little romance."

"Do you think people … notice that?"

"Judging by Mark J.'s text, yes. Although, I think Mark J.'s a habitual caller-in. One time he started reading his poetry, when all I was looking for was an answer to a trivia question. Needless to say, I now leave the giveaways to the day hosts."

"So, you don't think it's weird that people … know?"

"What, that we kissed? Or that I like you?" I shake my head. "No, it's not weird. I mean, I want to take you out and do the sorts of things kids these days do for dates. I'm a fairly private person, but I don't want to hide away. I like you, and I want people to know that."

"I do, too," she says quietly.

"Are you worried about Ezra and Prudence?"

She pales, and I know that's the case.

"I'm not going to let either one near you. The second they involve you or Tonnie, this thing leaves my hands and goes to somebody else. I'll find someone not under their thumbs. I'll take my findings to anyone and everyone who will listen, including the media." I can hear my various ex-girlfriends in my head, taunting me. Reminding me of what I already know. I drop my head in my hands and try to dispel it all. "I don't mean to be so obsessed, Kinley."

"John," she whispers, hesitantly. Her chair squeaks, then I hear her roll even closer to me. She places her hands over mine, forcing me to look at her. "Ezra Abel and that church of his ... they've taken over your life and ruined it. I can't—*won't*—ever begrudge you for thinking so much about them. I don't know how it hasn't consumed you entirely."

"I think it will all be better once I've taken him down," I say slowly, looking into her pretty eyes. Sometimes I think my soul has been fading piece by piece since the day my dad was diagnosed with ALS. But now that Kinley is my life, I think my soul is repairing itself. "But sometimes ... sometimes I fear I won't be able to turn any of this off. It'll just stay with me."

"It won't," she says, her voice quiet but clear. She leans in, brushing her lips against mine. "It won't."

I snake my hands down her arms, massaging my way to her hips. I pull her as close as our chairs will allow so I can deepen the kiss. Kissing her feels as if I've finally found a purpose—my *right* purpose. It feels as though I'm exhaling all of the bad in my life, then inhaling all of the bright spots that give it meaning.

She sighs, making my heart pound throughout my body—places where it definitely shouldn't be pounding while I'm in my workplace.

I pull away, reminding myself that a little later

somebody else will be sitting in these chairs, and smile at her. "Thank you for saying that."

"It's all the truth," she tells me. "You just have to have more faith in yourself."

"I think you put too much faith in me," I say.

"Someday, when all this is finished, I really hope you remember this conversation."

"That's an odd thing to say," I tell her. "Why would I forget any of our conversations?"

She only smiles at me, then points to a switch. "Tell me how all of this works."

CHAPTER 10

Kinley

I'm on a mission from the very second I enter the house. Michelle is standing in the kitchen, seemingly contemplating a cookbook I sincerely hope she's not planning on using. Parishioners gift her with cookbooks because they're so fooled into thinking she's a good cook. We end up stacking them on a bookshelf next to the pantry, occasionally dusting them so they appear used.

She glances up at me, hair falling from the braid she has it in. Other than that, she's wearing a pair of teal pants and a white knit sweater.

"Where's Prudence?" I ask.

Michelle blinks, looking at the door leading to the other rooms. "I think she's upstairs."

"Thank you," I say, then march past Michelle. If Michelle says anything else, I don't hear her. I'm too focused on finding my sister and reaming her.

Despite all of Ezra's attempts, I hoped I was molding her into a smart, mature, *kind* woman. Everything I've ever done has been so she would have the best chance at life, yet here she is proving that none of it mattered.

Somewhere, she became selfish and conceited, willing to exploit others for game. She wasn't just toying with John and me to please Ezra, she was doing it out of *enjoyment*.

The thing is, I'll bet Ezra would've made her step down if he knew how much improvement I'd made with John. But, really, what improvement am I making? My heart is just tangled up with all of Ezra's expectations, Prudence's games, and the feelings I have for John. I went into this hoping to give Ezra what he wants so Prudence would be safe, but now ... now John's safety is just as important to me.

And right now, the only problem that I can really see is Prudence. She can ruin everything and I wouldn't put it past her to do exactly that.

I find her in her room, lying on her daybed. Her room is a bright yellow, looking less like it belongs to a teenager verging on adulthood and more to a child. Her bedspread is a white quilt with lace sewn into it. Her room is what you would expect to see in a Barbie Dreamhouse catalog—another attempt to make it seem as if we're a perfect household, even though Prudence is the farthest thing from a doll.

When I walk in, she sets down a notebook she's scribbling in. Somewhere in the room, I can hear the radio playing, no doubt on John's station.

"Home from sinning, I see," she says with a smile that is both demure and merciless.

"Prudence, whatever you're doing, please stop."

She places her hand over her heart. "Whatever *I'm* doing? Dear sister, I'm only doing what I'm told. You're the one who can't seem to do what Ezra says."

"If you believe that, then let's tell him about the scene you made this afternoon," I say slowly, trying to gauge her reaction. All I want to see is some sort of remorse or regret, but I don't even see self-preservation.

Her lips tug into a tight smile, eyes glinting wickedly. "Then we'll also let him know what you're doing with

John. Talking on the radio alongside him? You know he's out to ruin us. He wants to stop Ezra's work."

"Oh, Prudence, why are you talking like that? You know it's all nonsense."

"Maybe, but Ezra has a rouse to keep up, doesn't he? Besides, that's not all I'd have to tell him. It seems to me that John's not the only one who's being toyed with. It might just be my imagination, but I sense feelings are being caught." The *t*-sound is so sharp, I flinch. She works her jaw, gearing up for verbal battle. "I knew it."

"Why do you even care, Prudence? You know I'm just doing this for you."

She rolls off the bed and stands, crossing her arms. "Are you? Because from where I stand, this has all been for yourself. I don't need you anymore. I haven't needed you in a long time. *You've* needed *me*. Without *me*, Ezra would've kicked you out a long time ago. As far as I'm concerned, we're all better off if you leave the family. It's not like you have any real importance."

"You don't mean that."

"It would be easier to tolerate you if you weren't so self-righteous."

There's so much venom in her icy glare—a snake about to bite. I've always been able to tell her anything, but over the last few years it's changed. Everything she says to me feels dangerous, and everything I say back is a potential testimony she can use against me later. She's always lying in wait for me to fall into a trap, and I've done exactly that by caring about John.

"I'm sorry," I say slowly, keeping my face devoid of emotion. "I will do my best to stay out of your way from now on. I would appreciate it if you wouldn't tell Ezra about what you think is going on between John and I. All that's happening is I'm getting closer to him to learn more information. In return, I won't tell Ezra that you nearly ruined everything today by using all of the information I've told you and the family confidence. I'm sure neither of us wants him to be the judge of our *betrayals*."

"No, we don't." Her chin raises. "But don't confuse my submission for fear. I do not fear Ezra."

"You should," I warn.

She chuckles, the tone cold. "I want what he has—I want his legacy. If anyone should be feared, it's me."

"Prudence ..." I trail off, deciding to leave our conversation at that and prepare to leave the room. When I'm halfway out, she calls after me, "You wouldn't be so angry with me if everything was just an *assumption*."

"Just like you wouldn't be so defensive if you weren't jealous."

I shut her door quickly, not wanting to start the conversation all over again. Prudence doesn't measure battles by who laid out the best arguments. She measures them in terms of who had the last word.

Michelle appears at the end of the hall. "Is everything all right, Kinley?"

I try to hold back my surprise. Is she actually showing some care toward me? I've done enough lying lately, and Michelle won't judge me for being honest. I didn't realize it until now, but even though she's lost in her hazy world, she's the most real person in this family. I've just never paid any attention because she's so bleary.

"No, it's not," I say in a whisper, messing with the cuffs of my sweater. I stare at the ground as I create some space between Prudence's door and I. "I knew Prudence changed, but I didn't know how much."

"She's definitely formed herself in Ezra's ... shadow." She makes a gesture, looking off into the distance. "Just as much as you've formed the opposite of his shadow."

"I haven't ... I'm still doing what he wants." I bite my lip because the words I say next practically spring out. "Do you ever wish you could escape him?"

"I'm here, aren't I?" she says, a pleasant smile on her face. I can't tell what she's trying to say, although it's clear it has a special meaning to her. So maybe I'm sort of wrong about her being the most honest—she's truthful in her own way, but you need a key to decipher her. "He wants to see you in his office."

"Okay," I say. *Lucky me.* "Thank you for letting me know."

I start down the stairs, but she says my name. "Tell him about your sister before she tells him about you."

"We agreed—" I cut off, knowing she's right. Agreements don't mean anything between Prudence and me. I can't trust her, and because of that, she's can't trust me. No matter what, one of us is going to pull the trigger on the truth, and I have to be the one to do it first because I have the most to lose.

But how do I tell him?

Ezra's office is a room on the back of the house that used to be a screened breezeway. It's one of the few additions made to the house, mainly because Ezra wanted to switch out the screens for windows. It's one of the few things I can relate to about him—he finds calm in nature. But he also uses it as a tactic for impressing parishioners and important people. Ezra's made it so every part of his life can be idolized by somebody.

He's watering the large, fiddle leaf plant beside his mahogany desk, practicing his next sermon. Halfway into a sentence, his brow furrows and he scribbles something on a paper. Sometimes I wonder if his monetary ambitions were removed, if he'd make a good preacher. But he's not the type of person to do anything without reward.

He must've heard me enter, because he holds up two fingers, squeezing his eyes shut. Something seems to come to him, because he starts nodding his head, then scratching and scribbling on the paper again.

After a minute, he straightens, flattening his palms on the desk top. "Prudence tells me you didn't do as I said."

Michelle and I were wrong; Prudence was faster than we expected. Any last shred of hope that my sister might still love me shrivels up like a fallen dead leaf.

He waits, and I take that as him expecting me to say something. Honestly, I generally don't speak around him because that's the safest route, so I'm not used to his cues. I don't know when I can test his limits versus when he wants me to talk versus when I had better keep my mouth shut.

"She's telling you the truth," I admit. "From what I've learned about him, he's someone who needs time. Prudence and I can't change his mind overnight. I know her tactics might work with other people, but John has principals ... and I think that Prudence knows that. All she's doing is coming on too strong and poisoning him against—"

Ezra pinches the bridge of his nose, silencing me with the motion. I don't need a cue to know I was talking too much.

"I can already see you're telling the truth, also," he says, slowly. "You've always been better at understanding people. I had just hoped this would all be tied up by now."

"From what he's told me, he doesn't have any immediate plans. He's only collecting information."

"He's still collecting information despite what Prudence believes?"

I consider lying, but I nod. Ezra isn't naive enough to believe otherwise.

"Damn it," he mutters. "He might not have plans now, but there's no telling what he might do if he finds anything. Have you figured out the point behind this vendetta of his yet?"

My cheeks heat up. This is entirely Ezra's fault, but I'm terrified he'll blame someone else. "John's dad ... you did a healing on him."

"So he was a plant? What's that got to do with anything?"

"No, he wasn't a plant. He was dying and his family pulled together their funds to pay you to heal him, except you couldn't and you blamed him."

"Of course I blamed him," he bites out, a vein pulsing in his neck. Otherwise, he manages to remain calm. "Who, in their right mind, honestly believes a human can heal another human? It's all purely psychological. I can't really heal cancer or—what did he have?"

"ALS."

"Or ALS."

My heartbeat feels slower and I feel dizzy, odd considering the burst of adrenaline I had when I volunteered to research John. But this time is different because I can see John's pained expression as he told me … I can hear the tremor to his otherwise strong voice as he spoke about losing his dad. I feel as though I'm swimming upstream, against a rapid current of John's words and Ezra's demands and false claims.

"This is why some people deserve to have their money taken from them and given to others who will use it right," he continues.

A knock sounds at the door, followed by Prudence's voice, "Daddy?"

I glance over my shoulder at her, which earns me a smile that makes her look as if she's won something. The smile fades almost immediately when Ezra says, "Not now, Prudence." Her jaw drops a little, but she recovers quickly and goes back to smiling. Little does she know that she didn't do anything to help her case.

When she's gone, he starts going through an orderly stack of papers on his desk. Eventually he gives up and pulls a key from a drawer. It goes to a filing cabinet behind him. He searches until he finds exactly what he's looking for.

He holds out a piece of paper, with his *Ezra Abel* signature, but also a signature for a *Jacob Taylor Abelson* in his writing. I stare blankly at it, not sure what it means.

"We'll make a copy of that and you will give it to him. Come up with whatever you think will fit the story you've already told him. We'll see what he does with the information he finds."

"I'm sorry, but what exactly is this?" I ask.

He almost looks burdened that I don't somehow know without being told. "I had my name changed shortly before I married Michelle. The only record of it was removed a few years ago by a friend. However, this will lead him to an arrest record from when I was nineteen— petty theft. It's a story I can spin to fit my narrative, but this will at least be a controlled test to see what he'll do given damning information."

I don't want to ask, but I gather up the courage and do it anyway. "And if he does do something?"

"Then we find damning information on him or create it."

#

I'm not sure what I'm doing until I'm on the bus and dialing John's number. I don't want to do what Ezra's asking me to do. I just want to see John. He brings normalcy to my life, and I'm beginning to rely on that. I didn't realize how much I needed it.

The photocopy Ezra gave me is folded neatly in my purse where I hide my tampons so John doesn't somehow happen upon it. Ever since I met him I've been meeting a series of forks in the road, and here I am at another one. Do I lie to John or lie to Ezra? Unfortunately, it's easier to lie to John right now, no matter how much it hurts.

John answers on the third ring. "Kinley?" he says groggily.

"Did I wake you?" I ask in a rush. It's one in the afternoon; I should've thought about the fact that John works nights. He's probably tired. I know I am after pulling the all-nighter with him at the radio show.

"No, I just nodded off," he says. "Hearing your voice makes waking up worth it. Damn, that was cheesy, wasn't it? Call it tiredness."

"I'm sorry," I apologize.

"Hey, no, you're fine. You're fine. I probably wasn't going to sleep long anyway. Is everything okay?"

"Yes—no. I don't know. I was thinking about the church and … and I think I found something."

"That fast? Wow."

"I called in a favor," I lie. I'm glad he can't see my flaming cheeks and feel my sweaty palms. "One of the community theater actors is a government employee." I hope it's a lie he buys, considering I've been practicing it; I've also been practicing telling John the truth. I'm somehow both ready for anything and nothing at the same time.

"Clearly all I've needed is a Kinley," he says, and I can only imagine his grin. "Why don't you head on over to my place?"

"I already am. I should be there in about ten minutes."

"Looking forward to it. I'll meet you at the stop." He pauses, as if he has something else to say.

"John?"

"Sorry, I just—I had a strange feeling is all."

"What kind of strange feeling?" *Does he know?*

"This is the first time I've been more excited about something other than finding information on the church. I'm more excited to see you than I am to hear what you have to say."

My heart simultaneously picks up speed and turns cold—I'm making the wrong decision. I can't hurt John. I just don't know how to fit him into the equation to make everything work out.

"Anyway," he says, most likely taking my silence to mean something else, "I'll let you go."

"Okay," I whisper.

I hang up the phone and set it in my lap, noticing that a male passenger is eyeing me closely. I'm sure watching me was an emotional roller coaster and he doesn't even know the half of it. Luckily, the passenger gets off at the next stop instead of trying to have an awkward conversation about the call.

Time passes fast and, suddenly, before I know it, it's my stop and I see John waiting for me, wearing a gray jacket and khakis, hands stuffed in his pockets.

I grab my purse and hurry out to him, noting how pale his cheeks are and how red his nose and ears are.

"You don't need to meet me," I tell him as I come to a halt.

"Sure I do," he says, reaching out to mess with the collar of my peacoat.

"You'll catch a cold."

He chuckles. "That's an old wives' tale." He leans into me, pressing his icy lips against mine, somehow managing to create instant warmth. Since our first kiss, he's surprised me with tiny kisses here and there, but this one feels real and more like the first one. Like it counts.

He moves his hand from my jacket to the back of my neck, while he slips the other down to the small of my back, pulling me closer to him. I move into him willingly, cupping his cheeks with my own hand. His tongue flicks against my lips and I gasp in surprise, giving him the room to deepen the kiss.

He pulls back with a raspy chuckle, wrapping his arm around my waist and guiding me toward his apartment. "What a greeting," he says. He brushes his lips against my temple. "From now on, I'm meeting you every time."

I blush, then lean my head onto his shoulder. We could walk straight into a pack of hyenas and I don't think either of us would blink. "I think I understand why you do that now."

He grins down at me. "Glad you're catching onto my nefarious ways."

After we get up to the apartment and calm down Clancy, I take a spot on the couch, with her head on my lap. John sits down beside me, after grabbing a beer for himself and glass of tea for me.

I take a sip and then reach into my purse. "This isn't much."

"If it's something I don't have," he says slowly, eying my purse, "then it's something important."

I open the tampon pocket, careful he doesn't catch a glimpse, then set my purse aside once I have the letter out. I open it and hand it to him. He looks over it with the same confusion I probably had.

I point to Ezra's name now, followed by his real name. "He hasn't always been Ezra Abel. He changed his name," I explain.

His jaw drops and he pulls it closer, as if he can't quite make out the words, even though Ezra's large, flowing cursive is very legible. "Jacob Taylor Abelson," he says slowly. "How the hell did he come up with Ezra?"

I wish I knew the answer to that, as well. There is *The Book of Ezra,* but that is in no way related to Ezra's way of preaching. "Maybe he thought it sounds important?"

He sets the paper on Clancy's head, which earns him a heavy sigh from the disagreeable pup. "This opens up a whole ... wow. Who knows where this might lead, Kinley. You really came through. I don't know how to thank you—or that friend from the theater." He closes his eyes, leaning his head back against the couch. "God, I can't even tell you what this means to me. I've been looking for so long and coming up with nothing."

I hate myself. *Hate* isn't even a strong enough word. All I can do is frown, glad he's not looking at my expression. I don't know what to say, because nothing will ever be fair to him. *I'm* the one with nefarious intentions. He'll never forgive me if he ever finds out, and I can't blame him. I don't deserve forgiveness.

"What do you think you'll do next?" I ask in a barely-there voice.

He's too happy to notice that I'm pulling back. He just opens his eyes and links his hands at the back of his head, staring straight up at the ceiling.

"I'm not sure. I guess I'll look into this, see what I find, talk to you and Tonnie. If it comes up with anything major … I'm really not sure. I've been planning to bring him down for so long, that I don't know what I'll do when I have the chance to follow through with it."

I like that answer. I trust that answer. That's an answer even Ezra will buy.

"Do you want to look into it now?" I ask.

He looks at me, then at his laptop, then back to me. He tucks a strand of hair behind my ear, then runs his hand along my scar. I can't help but shiver. My hands are the only hands that have ever touched it. I've always been so afraid people might find it repulsive—the way the skin is riddled with little creeks and valleys.

"No, I don't. I think I just want to spend time with you," he says, almost in awe.

"You sound surprised."

"I am," he explains. "Normally I'm so focused on the church I don't make time for other people. The last few girls I've dated—I liked them, but I didn't *care*. I've been so involved with my research, I guess I've gotten a little lost in it. With you …"

He trails off, but I know what he's saying. "I feel the same way," I whisper. I wish I could tell him that I've always done what Ezra says, all because of Prudence. But here, lately, I'm fighting that instinct. I think if I had more courage, I would choose to do what's best for John over my sister. She's begun to feel like a lost cause—like the only way to save her, even if it means making her hate me forever, is to end all of this. Maybe I really, truly should be on John's side.

John leans closer to me and Clancy jumps down and moves away, almost as if she can sense what's happening.

The second his lips touch mine, we fall back to where we were on the street corner. This time the kiss deepens faster, a delicious mixture of languidness and hastiness—awakening my nerve endings and sending shock waves throughout my bloodstream. *This* must be what it is like to be healed.

John twines his hand through mine and gives a simple tug, which I follow through with willingly. I don't know where he's pulling me to, but I'll let him, so long as the kiss doesn't end.

He settles me on his lap so my legs are on either side of his thighs. He presses his hands into my hips, snaking his fingers up beneath my sweater, resting his palms on the waistband of my pants. He slips so easily into this arrangement, my mind starts reeling for a brief, chaotic moment.

What do I do with my hands?

I settle for putting a hand on his shoulder, the other at his neck. I'm sure I shouldn't be thinking this much—I should just be letting myself go with the flow—but how can I do that when I don't exactly know what the "flow" is?

Sometimes I swear he can hear my thoughts because he pulls away, kissing down my jawline toward my neck. He pauses at my ear to murmur, "Relax, Kin."

I arch my neck, finding that relaxation when his tongue tortuously flicks against the middle of my scar—awakening it and soothing it.

"You're free with me," he says, this time pulling back to look at me.

I answer him by initiating my own kiss. That earns me a grin I can't see but can feel.

He slowly roams his hands up my ribcage, drawing my shirt up. "Is this okay?" he asks, searching my gaze.

I bite my lip. "I'm just … nervous." I sit back slightly, trying to hold back a momentary bit of surprise when I feel him hard against my core. My stomach tightens, wanting something I can't understand. Ezra has never been quiet about his sex life with Michelle when he's telling Prudence to talk men into things. It's a subject Ezra places a double standard on—sex is not to be spoken about unless it's his sex life or ends to a means.

No, I won't think about Ezra.

There's a fire in John's eye as he watches me release my lip, but he holds back. "This is all new to you."

"Yes," I admit. "And my scar …"

"Is beautiful," he tells me, raining a few kisses along my cheek. He pulls away when he's proven his point. "Keep going or stop?"

I close my hands over his. "A little further," I tell him, then help him pull my sweater off. "This far."

I'm not ready to show him what's underneath my modest, plain bra. As it is, you can see that the scar extends down into it, but I don't want him to see the rest. The fire ruined the skin on my breast, barely leaving my nipple behind. The scar travels further down, ending at the middle of my ribcage. Most of my nerve damage is in that area.

"Okay," he says. "But we'll make it even."

He leans back to take off his own shirt, revealing his tanned chest, all angles and muscles. A faint trail of blondish hair runs over and between his pecs, with another trail leading from his belly button to the top clasp of his jeans. I feel a little like a fool, eyes almost glazed over as I watch him. Enamored, I place my hand on one of his abs and push. Cut like stone.

He laughs, then takes my hand in his. "Lean back for a second. Want to show you something."

Even though his body clearly wants more, he's doing exactly as he said. *He's a gift,* I think to myself, wondering how I deserved him.

I do as he says and he leads my hand down to his left side, just above his jeans. There's a small crater there, rough and whiter than the rest of his skin.

"When I was a stupid kid, I thought I was invincible or something. Some friends and I used to sneak out to some woods, just down the street from here—see who could climb the highest. I didn't want to look like a wussy, so I climbed a huge one. I impressed all my friends, but I also fell and impaled myself on a rock. The doctors said it was a miracle I didn't rupture anything." He leaves my hand alone in that spot to lay his against my cheek. "We all have scars, Kinley. Don't be afraid to show me yours because of how you think I'll react. If anything, I think they make you gorgeous and strong."

I smile at him, my shoulders finally losing some of their tension. "You say the best words."

"So we're on the same page, then?"

"Yes," I say.

"Good deal," he says.

His lips brush mine again, but the kiss doesn't move any further than where we're at now.

CHAPTER 11

John

I'm sitting in one of the pews, my notebook on my knee, listening to Ezra preach. Halfway through a sermon about children and homelessness, he points into the audience, his long arm extending in my direction.

"John Smith, please come to the stage," he commands.

I'm so surprised, I stand automatically. I look to my left, toward the aisle, and I'm struck dumb by Kinley and Tonnie beside me. Kinley looks at me with hopeful tears in her eyes, while Tonnie beams.

"This will work," Tonnie tells me, reaching across Kinley to touch my cheek.

Kinley stands on her tiptoes. "It has to," she says, then presses her lips against my cheek. "I can't lose you."

Lose me?

Everyone is staring at me, suffocating me. Ezra's voice booms over the crowd. "John Smith, join me on the stage now."

Somehow, someway, I walk. Am I finally taking him down? Is that what they meant?

I hear footsteps behind me, followed by Kinley's sniffles. They're following me? If my head was on straight and in the here and the

103

now, I'd tell them to leave me to this. I don't want them involved. Except I can't. It's as if I'm under someone—something—else's control.

I don't stop walking until I've made my way up the stairs and to the edge of the stage, just in front of Ezra. He stands in front of me, taller than I expected, casting a shadow as if he's my judge.

"What are you here to request of God?"

What? Why am I doing this? Am I trying to prove him wrong? My mouth opens and I don't even recognize the words that leave my lips. "I need to be healed."

"What is your ailment?"

"ALS," I say.

It has to be a lie, right? I'm walking and I feel fine. Normal. I know what it looks like because I watched it wreck my dad. I can't have it.

But something tells me I do. A small voice—the same small one that forced me up here.

"Are you ready to accept God into your heart and allow Him to heal you?" Ezra asks, his words thundering through the church, raising his hands as if he's praising himself. But his hands freeze mid-air and he sneers, almost growling, "No. This is wrong. You can't be healed. You can't accept God—you don't believe. You're sick because you can't open your heart. The only thing left for you is death ..."

"John." Kinley. Her voice is urgent, and I suddenly feel her tugging on my arm. "John, you're just dreaming. You're okay."

I open my eyes to find her wild-eyed, laying on the couch in front of me and tucked in my iron-clad hold. After a while we stopped kissing, I made an excuse to finish myself off in the bathroom and I held her while we talked. Nothing church-related, just off-the-wall things we both had to say. She asked me more about my childhood and I told her my funny stories, which got her to open up a little about her childhood. I guess I must've dozed off somewhere in all of that.

Shit, the last thing I wanted was to fall asleep on her. Not just because it's rude, but because I have nightmares. They're what keep me up most days and the reason why I work best off so little sleep. Usually it's just that day of the healing for my dad, but this was different. It was me, and it felt so real.

I squeeze my eyes shut. I feel childish, as if I'm going to burst into tears. "Sorry. I didn't want you to see that. God, I can't even sleep without him ruining everything."

"You're talking about Ezra?"

"Yeah. It's that day in the church—I just keep reliving it."

I slowly relax my muscles, then carefully move my arms so I'm not clutching onto her for life as I was. Clancy is between our legs. It's a good thing I have an ottoman attached to this thing or else we'd all roll off.

Kinley reaches up to my forehead and brushes at my hair, which is drenched in sweat from the nightmare. I feel feverish and my legs are restless. I stay still, knowing that she's trying to comfort me. She doesn't initiate a lot of contact unless I do first, so this means a lot. As embarrassed as I am about having a bad dream like a ten-year-old kid, I also want her to be comfortable with me.

"I hope that you find peace," she says quietly. "I can't imagine how that whole thing must weigh on you."

"Yeah," I say. "And I don't want other people to feel the same way I do."

She nestles her head into the pillows we're using. Being so close is not doing any wonders for my heartbeat, but it does make me feel calmer.

"Was it okay that I woke you up?" she asks. "You looked so panicked, but I know some people prefer to find resolutions ..."

"You did the right thing. Honestly, this dream was different, and it shook me. Not to sound like Dorothy from the *Wizard of Oz,* but you were there and so was Tonnie. It wasn't Dad getting reamed by Ezra—it was me.

I couldn't stop it. I was a dying man, and he blamed me for it. I've never …" I swallow and rest my forehead against hers. I close my eyes, unable to say the words while looking at her. I'll blubber like a fool. "I've never been able to put myself in his shoes. Just trying to think what he must've felt has always turned me into a wreck. I can't imagine how much the ALS had him suffering or how it felt to know you were going to die—how he stayed strong for us. And then for Ezra to trick him … I don't want to know what that did to him during his final few weeks before he passed."

She lets out a breath, smelling like a fresh pot of mint tea. "That would haunt me, too, John. But I can't believe your dad would have let Ezra Abel wreak havoc on his mind or faith. He had your love, plus everyone else's who knew him, and I'm sure that's what mattered." She smiles at me faintly. That smile is reassurance that there is a heaven. She's too angelic for there not to be. "And, as for your nightmare, you're here and healthy. You have to be so you can take down Ezra."

"With you, I feel like I can do anything," I tell her. Cheesy, but honest. "Can I … would you like to see a picture of my parents?"

The brightness of Kinley's grin is almost too much to look at directly. "I would love that."

"All right," I say. I move my feet a little bit, hoping Clancy will take the hint. She only growls. "Up, Clancy," I command, which gets her moving. She jumps down, waiting for the two of us to move. As soon as we're up, she takes the same spot on the couch. "I'll be right back."

I head back to my room, where I have the old photo albums my mom kept when I was a kid. When she passed, I stored them away at the back of my closet to collect dust. It's one thing to think about them, but it's another to see the memories I made with my parents. My heart shatters every time I realize there will be no more memory-making—all I have left are these pictures.

I pull out the box, searching for the one labeled *Wedding*. I find the one I'm thinking of—the one Mom used to have hanging in the hallway right when you walked into our house. Every year, she and my dad would pull it down, write a note to each other, and then stuff it in the back. They never actually read their notes, but Dad called it their *In-Case-of-Emergency-Please-Break* stash to remind them of why they loved each other. I used to think it was a stupid, gross tradition, but I wish I had those notes.

Instead, Mom put the ones she wrote for him in his casket before they buried him, then I did the same for her.

I rub at my face, figuring if Kinley's already seen me have a nightmare, she might as well see the rest of my soul. Who the hell cares if I get a little emotional, anyway?

When I walk back out, Kinley's stroking Clancy's ear, waiting patiently. She offers me a gentle smile as I sit down beside her and hand her the picture.

"Excuse my language, but it's one of those shitty glamour shots," I tell her. "But, God, they look happy."

"They do," she agrees. "They're immortalized."

My dad has his arms wrapped around my mom. He's wearing an ugly blue suit, his hair fluffed up in that flock of seagulls look. He's grinning from ear to ear, a twinkle in his eyes that always seemed to be there, even when he was sick. My mom looks like she's starting into, or finishing, a fit of laughter, but not in an awkward way. More candid and representative of how much she adored my dad. Her blonde hair is *almost* bigger than her puffy white sleeves, her blue eyes standing out next to my dad's suit.

"You have your dad's face but your mom's smile," Kinley says, tracing lightly over their faces.

"I've been told that." I put my arm on the back of the couch behind her and lean in. "My dad had a great sense of humor. He could make just about anyone laugh, while my mom would laugh at the drop of a dime. Needless to say, he constantly had her in a fit."

"I can tell," she says. "His smile is very mischievous."

"He was a very mischievous man. Even at the end."

"You can tell they loved each other very much."

"They did. You know, as much as I wish my mom was still here, I know she wouldn't have been happy without him. They were the love of each other's lives."

Kinley hands the photo back to me and says cautiously, "You don't talk about your mom very much."

"You noticed that, huh? I guess I sort of lose her in trying to find redemption for our family. But it's also harder to think about her passing than Dad. For most of my life, I knew he wasn't going to be around for very long. I knew I had to love him as much and as hard as I could so when the day came, I wouldn't regret anything. But Mom … I wasn't prepared. Her heart attack felt so random and so unfair. I'm not sure I'll ever accept it."

"I wish things had been easier for you."

"I wish they'd been easier for you, too." I lean forward to set the photo on the coffee table. "Just to lighten the mood with dark humor, but we could totally start an orphan club."

"That is very dark," she says with a laugh.

I can't help but kiss her, thankful that she's just, I don't know … Kinley. I pull away, glancing at the clock. Dinner is in my future, then work. "Do you want to join me for another show?"

#

I'm beginning to think Kinley doesn't have the best home situation. I thought it was weird that she didn't have a car, even weirder that she doesn't talk about her family, but it didn't really hit home until today that there's something wrong.

Whether I'm a grown-ass man or not, Tonnie literally demands I text her if I do anything out of the ordinary, so she knows I'm not—her words—"smelling like a day-old opossum roasting on asphalt." Family is supposed to suffocate you with love and fear for your general well-being.

Except Kinley only looked at her phone once through the course of our time together, grimaced, then put her phone away for good. If that was, say, over the course of a couple of hours, that'd be fine. She not only went into work with me and Clancy again, then she came home with us and slept there. We're nearing the twenty-four-hour mark of time together and nobody seems to care.

All this time I thought Tonnie was doing it right, but maybe she's just overprotective and caring. Who knows, but I want to give Kinley's family the benefit of the doubt. They could just trust her enough that they don't check in on her, and she might've checked in with them while I was around. I mean, they can't be bad people if they adopted Kinley and raised her into the woman she is.

All right, I'm definitely edging toward conspiracy theorist territory. First Ezra, now Kinley's family, next it'll be DB Cooper or Sasquatch.

Doing my best to shake those thoughts away, I start boiling noodles for the spaghetti I'm making for dinner. Kinley's still sleeping in my bedroom because, coincidentally, people other than me need sleep.

When we got back, she looked so tired and I felt like I could sleep, so I offered up another nap. This time, in my room. I thought it'd be weird, considering our relationship is still pretty new, but it felt so automatic to pull her into my arms and drift off. I didn't even have any bad dreams this time, though I'm sure it was a fluke. As perfect as Kinley may be—shady non-conversations with her family aside—she is not a cure for nightmares.

She walks into the kitchen, rubbing at her eyes will simultaneously sniffing the air. She's barefoot, as I am, and for a second I allow myself to believe we're at a far later stage in our relationship and she lives here. I just love how easy it feels to not be alone and to have someone—specifically *Kinley*—with me.

"Whatever you're making smells delicious," she says.

"Homemade spaghetti and meatballs."

"My stomach told me to tell you it loves you."

I chuckle. "It clearly has good taste." I motion over my shoulder for her to come closer. She leans around me to look at the pot, hand timidly on my back. I get a small spoonful of the sauce and hand it to her. "Tonnie told me to never eat anything without taste-testing it first."

"She's a true genius," Kinley says, then tries the sauce. She makes a little moaning sound that makes my heart go into overdrive and my body react in ways that'd make those beautiful cheeks of hers turn rosy. "Oh my goodness. That's amazing."

"It had better be—that's Velma's secret recipe," I tell her, taking the spoon back.

Food be damned, I put my hands on either side of Kinley's hips and lift her onto the island countertop. She giggles, resting her arms on my shoulders when she's situated. I stand between her legs, eye-level with her.

"Did you sleep okay?" I ask.

She nods. "Your mattress felt like heaven. Did you sleep … okay?"

"No nightmares, if that's what you're asking."

"You promise you're okay with me being here?"

She pulls her lip between her teeth, looking so genuinely worried, I can't help but lean in and kiss her. I take that same lip and pull it between my own teeth, before letting it go so I can kiss her deeply. If I could, I'd build a church and worship her. Beauty, kindness, innocence, brilliance—it's all in her.

My lips leave hers because I love how much she loves it when I kiss her scar. Tasting her skin is intoxicating as it is, but knowing that I am making her more comfortable with herself—I can't explain it. I wish it could be my purpose in this life.

"John," she says breathlessly, her nails digging into my back. But then she says, "Oh, John!" in an exclamation that is not because of anything I'm doing to her. "Something's burning."

"Shit," I say, bounding away from her and toward the oven. I pull a towel off the handlebar as I pull the oven further open. Luckily our garlic bread isn't quite charred, but most of the pieces are relatively burnt. We might get a good one each. I set the pan on the oven top, grimacing. "This is evidence of the way you fog up my head," I tell her. "Clearly I don't muddle yours up as much."

She laughs, jumping down from the counter. Clancy is hidden somewhere out of fear. Anything that is loud, smells funny, or is just plain strange—sometimes even normal—and she's out of the picture. You wouldn't even know I had a dog. But man oh man, if one of those people on the street tries to come in.

"That was survival instinct," she corrects. "I was very happy with what we were doing."

"Until the oven decided to turn it all to hell."

"How rude of the oven," she says.

She sets the table with forks and napkins, while I put our spaghetti on the plates with our single pieces of garlic bread. As I'm reaching for the wine bottle on my counter, I realize I don't even know Kinley's age. She looks young, but when you talk to her you realize she has an old soul.

"Are you legal to drink wine?" I ask, holding the bottle up.

She shakes her head.

My heart drops a little, her words echoing about Prudence being seventeen. I trust Kinley entirely, but there's so much I don't know about her and, like the lack of communication with her family, there's something off about her. I'm sure I'll know it with time, but she's just so reserved.

"Mind if I ask how old you are?"

"Nineteen," she answers.

Tonnie makes me watch *It's a Wonderful Life* every year, and in my head, I hear George Bailey say, "Why only last year you were sixteen." In this case, eighteen.

"And I'm twenty-five," I mutter. I slip the wine back into place, deciding I'll drink sweet tea with her instead. Later, if we're on the couch, I'll drink a beer, but it would be strange to sit across from her drinking and knowing she can't … because she's six years younger. Not a big gap, but enough.

"So when do you go into the retirement home?" she asks so sweet all I can do is stare at her blankly.

Finally, after her words settle in, I burst out into a hearty laugh. It's honestly the best laugh I've had in years. The more I get to know her, the more she opens up and surprises me.

"Thanks for that," I say.

"You seemed a little mortified."

"Six years isn't anything, really," I say, convinced it's the truth. I mean, sure we're separated by a generational name, but I'm sure our experiences have aged us both more than we're likely to admit. Sometimes I feel fifty, worn down by everything that's happened.

"Exactly," she agrees.

I set our plates down and we eat in comfortable silence. Eventually, when we've eaten most of our food, I realize I never answered her question. Sure, I kissed the hell out of her, but I didn't confirm anything. Knowing her, it's probably gnawing at her.

"Just in case you want clarification," I tell her, which earns me a shy, confused smile, "I'm more than happy you're here. I know we haven't been together long, but you … you mean a lot to me, Kin."

She looks down at her plate, blushing. "You mean a lot to me, too, John."

"You know, I don't want to sound self-deprecating or too sentimental, but I was beginning to believe I wasn't going to get too much happiness out of life. Then you came along, and I'm reconsidering everything I ever thought."

Her eyes are sparkling when she looks at me, and I swear I can see my feelings returned in their endless, evergreen depths. "John, I—"

Suddenly, a hand pounds on my door, which earns several ferocious barks from Clancy. She comes running into the room, ready to attack, although I doubt she'd do much given the opportunity.

Kinley and I exchange worried glances, her face pale, while my cheeks feel hot. *What the hell?* Honestly, my fear is it's going to be Ezra Abel's muscle, here to make it clear I need to buy in or get lost. The last thing I want is for him to do anything in front of Kinley. Shit, what if he hurts—

"John, it's me," Tonnie says through the door.

I jump up from the table and open the door. Tonnie is on the other side, looking frazzled, clothes rumpled and hair falling from its ponytail. She's also a little green, though there's also something close to fury in her eyes.

"What's wrong?" I immediately ask, mind spinning out of control.

"That—that girl!" she exclaims. "That daughter of that *damn* Ezra Abel, damn it all!" She continues on, saying basically the same thing, except with more curse words.

"Tonnie, calm down. You have to tell me what happened."

"I'll have to show you! I'm just so—so—" She throws her hands up, speechless.

I reach for Kinley's coat on the hook beside the door. "We'll walk over with you."

"Oh, Kinley," Tonnie says, holding a hand to her heart. "I'm so sorry you were dragged into all of this."

"What's Kinley got to do with it?" I ask.

"You'll see," Tonnie says.

"Tonnie, tell me," I demand, feeling ready to curse right along with Tonnie, plus rip and throw shit. Sure, Kinley said she'd help, but I refuse to let any of this cause her problems.

"No, you have to see," Tonnie tells me again, then

starts to walk away.

I hurriedly help Kinley into her coat, trying to be more gentleman than beast, then follow after Tonnie. Kinley's quiet behind me, pale as a ghost and shaking. I have half the mind to take her hand in mine.

When we get over to Tonnie's place, she has to unlock the door—an automatic warning that something's happened. Tonnie never closes the doors to the public if she's scheduled to be opened. Four of her employees are huddled at a table in the far corner, whispering amongst themselves. They're the first thing I notice, until one the woman who cooks the meals, Regina, looks at me, then scowls at the table Kinley and I sit at.

Written across the glass tabletop in red lipstick is, *If you fuck a liar, the liar will fuck you, John.* Salt and pepper are littering the tabletop and booth, plus anything else she could find to cause annoyance.

"Since we opened, we've never been vandalized once, but then this happens today," Tonnie says in a rush. "It's ... it's despicable for her to write *that* on my table—when I've never done anything to her—to *you* about Kinley."

"Did she do anything else?" I ask through my teeth, my molars grinding.

"She didn't pay her bill and she ran her lipstick across the furniture like a stick on a picket fence, but this was the worst of it. I don't know if I'm overreacting, but—"

"You're not. We should call the police."

"No, John, we can't."

"Why not?"

"Because it won't accomplish anything. There's no way of proving she did this. Only one of our waiters saw Prudence. He said he'd make a statement, but I don't think his statement would hold up. Ezra has way too many strings to pull in these types of situations."

"She's taunting us. She knows we won't do anything, Tonnie."

"She's a conniving little twit," Tonnie mutters. "God, if

I had been here, I would've kicked her ass out. Frankie was her waiter. He said she was here for an hour, ordering food she'd only complain about. He said she kept staring up at your apartment building, but he thought she was just looking for someone. It was slow, so he took a break to smoke, and when he came back she was gone and this was here. When Frankie described her, I had no doubt it was Prudence."

"Why the hell would she do this? There's no way Ezra told her to. It's too public. This is just her being immature, I'm sure of it. All because I said no to eating with her and haven't been texting her back." I turn my fists into a ball, my heart pounding in my ears. So this is how it feels to be territorial. "She might think she can bully me in the church, but she as hell can't outside of it. And to say that about Kinley when she doesn't even know her ... Kin?"

She's been so quiet, I almost worry she's run off when she doesn't answer. I turn around and she jumps back slightly. I didn't realize how close she was standing—with her front practically against my back. Her face is drained of color, her eyes all watery as she stares at the table.

"Hey, it's all right," I say, closing the space and wrapping my arms around her. She willingly lets me pull her against my chest. "I'm sorry she's involving you."

Kinley makes a sniffling sound, then says, "I'm sure she's just jealous."

"Yeah, but she has no right to write that or feel that way," I say.

"He's right, sweetheart," Tonnie adds, putting a hand on Kinley's back. "This has nothing to do with you. It's just some teenager's warped little mind."

"I can't imagine being raised by that man," I say, blood turning to ice at the thought. "I'm sure there's a strong case of nature versus nurture there."

Kinley pulls away, not meeting my eyes. "I'll help clean up."

"Oh, there's no sense in that," Tonnie says.

"I want to. And then I should probably be getting home."

"I thought you were going to go on the show with me again," I say, sounding more than a little let down.

"Tomorrow, maybe," she says, offering a smile.

"Yeah, right, tomorrow," I say. "Tomorrow will be a new day, anyway. Not really in the mood for anything after this. We're okay?"

"Definitely," she says, standing on her toes and kissing my cheek. "I'm not leaving yet, silly."

CHAPTER 12

Kinley

Once again, I'm bent on finding my sister, except this time she's at the dining room table with Ezra and Michelle. Ezra is dressed in a tie and dress pants, while Prudence is wearing a long-sleeved dress, and Michelle is in a nice blouse and pants. I usually don't know much about their schedule, but tonight they have a wedding. It's on a weeknight because it's only a vowel renewal ceremony.

For the first time in my life, I don't care if Ezra is in the room. Normally I try to stay quiet, anticipating what will frustrate him. Right now, I don't care, because *I* get to be the frustrated one.

"Prudence," I say, my voice eerily level.

I know John could tell that something was wrong, but he didn't know what. He probably thought I was bothered by what this "stranger" did. Maybe worried I will leave him for good. Except the truth is none of this has anything to do with him. No, this was about me and the fact that I was getting what she couldn't have. Using language she knew I hated, twisting the situation into something it's not, making me seem like my emotions about this are all one-

117

dimensional—this was her trying to *hurt* me.

I see straight through her act to who she really is. I've been too focused on saving her and making her a better person, all the while missing what she turned into.

"What do you think—" Ezra begins, but I talk over him. Oddly enough, he immediately withdraws.

"I know what you did, Prudence. You're lucky they didn't call the police. That was a vile, horrible thing to do."

Prudence smiles innocently. "And what you're doing isn't vile and horrible? You're the one toying with John's emotions. I'm just trying to show him who he's dealing with."

"No, you don't get to act like—"

"Like what? Like I'm telling the truth?" She stands, putting her hands on either side of her plate and leaning against the table. "You're *falling* for each other. That's was *not* your job here."

"And your job wasn't to act like a jealous child! You're just upset because I'm doing what you can't, and you're taking it out on them. Ezra gave me information to test him, and you know what, Prudence? He's not going to do anything with it. He's going to sit on it. But what you did—you could have ruined everything. You—"

"Stop!" Ezra commands, slamming a hand down on the table. "Sit down, *now.*" Prudence's eyes flare, but she does as he says. I do too, even though I really want to maintain my sudden disobedience. That wouldn't be smart, considering what Prudence just said about my feelings for John. I honestly think Ezra could care less about how I feel, but I don't want to give him reason to start. As long as he thinks I'm following along with his plan, he shouldn't have reason to pry me away from John.

"I want an explanation for this outburst now, Kinley," he continues.

"Why are you—" Prudence starts, but Ezra holds up his hand.

"I don't owe you any reason for my actions, Prudence,

but I will say this once and *only* once: your word means nothing, because your word is often a lie. Now, Kinley."

Prudence's jaw drops and I have to take a second to hide my own astonishment. I knew Ezra didn't particularly like me, but I also thought he had some sort of an understanding with Prudence. I guess that's not the case.

"She's left a message for me at John's aunt's diner. It was very … colorful. She also took lipstick to the diner's furniture. It was red, so most of it bled when we tried to clean it and is permanent now. She made a mess with the condiments, too."

Ezra sits back in his chair, eyes squeezed shut and his jaw ticking. I know he's not going to blow up, because that's a part of his trade. He never loses control. Meanwhile, Michelle is over in her chair, eating as if nothing is happening.

Eventually, he sits forward, pointing a long, condemning finger at Prudence. "I have always said that no matter what, everything that we do must *not* lead back to me or the church. But this … I raised you better than this. This could have easily been the beginning of the end for us. You reacted instead of thinking, all because of what … childish jealousy? I told you to back down repeatedly, and you've failed to do that."

"I'm sorry," she says, seemingly folding into herself.

"That doesn't make up for what you've done. If this happens again, so help me God, I will make the next year of your life hell, then kick you out the second you turn eighteen. Do you understand me?"

"Yes, sir."

He turns to me for my rearing. "And if you ever disrespect me again, no matter what your sister's done, I will forget every promise I've ever made to you. I refuse to be drug into whatever selfish feud the two of you are in." He scoots his chair out and stands. "We'll be leaving now."

#

After they leave, I go up to my room and sit listlessly in my room, trying to figure out what I should do.

I wish I had a Tonnie of my own to talk to, but I don't.

Prudence has done a lot of wrong lately, but she was right when she said I'm falling for John. *Hard.* Enough that I want to be free to be with him. So free, in fact, that I came close to admitting the truth to him right before Tonnie came over.

I can't keep living this lie, but I know he won't let me back into his life once he knows the truth. After his comment about Prudence being Ezra's daughter, I doubt he could ever love me knowing Ezra raised me also. My life is filled with just as many wrongdoings as Prudence's. In fact, I've done more to make the presentation of the church and its healing seem real than she ever has. I'm more culpable in this mess.

Maybe if I can show him that his cause means more to me than church, then he won't react as badly when he finds out the truth. Instead of doing Ezra's bidding, I'll try to help John as much as I can. It's not like I can do anything to help Prudence anymore; it's clear from the way she's trying to destroy my happiness that she doesn't want me in her life helping her. I'm beginning to think she might not want me, period.

I head downstairs to look for the key to the church. On the ring is also a key to his office, where he stores files in a locked safe. While they're gone, maybe I can figure out the code. There might be something that's enough to help John. Something real, not given to me as a test.

The keys aren't very well hidden, because Ezra's never cared if we have them. Sometimes I take them to go to the church early to work on lighting or sound, or Prudence will prepare for an event. His safe code, though, won't be so easy. It's *highly* unlikely he'll use any of the codes most fathers would use—his anniversary, his wife's birthday, his daughters' birthday. If those documents put him at fault in any way, the safe will be impenetrable.

I slip on a pair of boots and my coat, then brave the cold walk to the church. It's snowing a little bit, so there's a dusting on the ground. It's enough to make me wish I would've chosen to do this mission at a more reasonable time or at least with a scarf or gloves. But you can't plan spontaneity, can you?

That sounds similar to something John would say, so I'm proud of myself for thinking it. He's a positive person, and I need his influence in my life.

As I'm approaching the church, I notice there's an African American woman dressed in a black coat and heels, but no stockings. She's yelling something into the icy wind, her whole body undulating with her stream of words.

"—Gone! He's gone, and you promised … you promised he would be all right! You said he was … cured …"

"Excuse me, ma'am," I say, walking toward her. "Ma'am," I say a little louder when she keeps yelling at the church. "Ma'am!"

The woman turns to look at me, makeup splashed down her cheeks as a result of her tears. Her eyes are frantic, seeming to look everywhere at once. There's so much heartache in her expression, but also raw, ugly anger. The second her gaze collides with mine, it all washes away, as if she was under a spell. Her shoulders droop and she puts her face in her hands.

"I'm sorry," she sobs. "I'm so sorry."

I don't know what to do, but I try to channel John again. I slowly move toward her, then wrap my arms around her. She falls into the hug, shivering and sobbing so hard it takes all my strength to hold us up.

"There's nothing to be sorry for," I say, rubbing circles into her back.

Eventually, she calms down and pulls away, dabbing at

her eyes and nose with her coat sleeve. "You're a complete stranger, and I just … today's been horrible. I hope you can understand."

"Of course I can." John's words the day we met come back to me—how he thought I looked lost so he invited me to the diner. "How about we walk across the street for a coffee? Or hot chocolate?"

"I shouldn't—"

"Please."

She nods. "I think I might need a stranger's kindness right now."

We walk over to a small, privately owned coffee house across the street. Neither of us talks while we order or wait for our drinks, so by the time we sit down at a table it's a little awkward.

Now that we're out of the cold and in the light, I can tell that she's maybe ten years older than me. She's one of the classiest women I've ever seen, despite the scene she was giving outside the church—with a sleek, black dress underneath her coat and diamonds on her ears, neck, wrists, and fingers.

I try not to focus on the stories people tell during the healings, especially when I know they're real, but the faces sometimes stick in my mind. Hers was recent—within maybe the last year. I don't remember anything beyond that.

She takes a small sip of the macchiato she ordered before clearing her throat. "I can't believe I did that. I'm acting foolish. I've just been such a mess. Today is the anniversary of my husband's death and I haven't been thinking straight."

"How could you be?" I ask. "I can't imagine how I would feel if I lost someone I loved."

"It's unimaginable. I've never known anyone to die— all but one of my grandparents are still alive, but she died before I was born. I never thought in a million years the first person I'd lose would be … Ca-Calvin." A tear slips out, but she quickly brushes it away, then takes another sip of her drink. Probably to distract herself. "Today has been the hardest day of my life."

"I lost my parents when I was younger. I don't remember much, but it's terrifying and heartbreaking when I think about the hole in my life that exists without them."

"And Calvin will definitely leave behind a hole. I've loved that man since we were twelve ... and ..." She trails off, smiling slightly. "I've barely talked to anyone—not even my mom—since he passed a few days ago, but here I am talking to you."

"It's easier. It's like a practice for when talking really matters."

"Well, even if this is practice, this conversation matters so much to me. This will stay with me for the rest of my life." She suddenly holds out her hand. "I can't believe I didn't introduce myself, I'm Althea."

"I'm Kinley." I shake her hand. I nervously spin my cup before I ask, "What led you to yell at that church?"

The anger from before storms over her expression and she looks over my shoulder, even though it's too dark to see the church right now.

"I know it probably sounds ridiculous, but ... that church had represented hope for us. My husband had a heart condition and he needed a transplant. It's such a terrible place to be in, because you want your husband to receive the call about that heart, but at the same time you realize that someone has to die for that call to be made. We got two calls, both of which fell through for different reasons. By then his body had already rejected a few other options we'd tried." She lets out a long breath, then starts fiddling with her necklace. "We'd attended the Church of Life a few times before, so we thought we might give the healing a chance. We did, and Ezra ... he said he healed him. I wouldn't have believed it except Calvin looked so wonderful. He had color in his cheeks and he wasn't breathing as heavily. He was actually awake and lucid. He removed himself from the transplant list. Looking back, it was all psychological—maybe even his final push to the end. But if Ezra wouldn't have lied to us, then he wouldn't … at the grocery store … gone …"

"I'm so sorry that happened to you and your husband."

She manages to regain her composure, but I can't tell she's barely hanging on. "I know I should've forced him to stay on the list. I know that staying on the list wouldn't have probably even meant anything. I know that Ezra Abel isn't the reason my husband died. But he's the reason why my heart had hope and now feels pulverized. He's the reason why I can't breathe—why I feel like I died on the grocery store floor, also." Tears start to fall again, and I reach for her hand. "We were supposed to have kids. We were going to run with the bulls for one of our milestone anniversaries. We were supposed to grow old together and drink beer on the front porch every night. We were supposed to …"

She buries her head in her free arm, murmuring more.

"Althea, Althea," I say, squeezing her hand. "Please look at me."

She does, all tears and emotion … but also survival.

"Everything you just said … I think we were supposed to meet. No, whether there's is a higher being or if it's just the universe, I *know* you were supposed to have the courage to tell me about your husband and I was supposed to have the heart to listen. I—I know somebody who has a similar story, except it was his father who passed. He's working to bring the church down. He's going to make what's happened to Calvin and his dad stop for good, so nobody else feels this way ever again."

I tell her about John and what he's been doing. As I do, she stares at me, eyes growing wide. Even though I've told her something amazing, her features grow tense. "That can't be true," she says when I've finished.

I blink. "It *is* true."

"H-how?" she stutters. "I didn't realize anyone would

be brave enough…" She trails off, shaking her head.

"I think you would be brave enough," I tell her.

She responds with an unsteady laugh. "I guess I was just giving the front of that church hell."

I smile. "You were."

"Losing somebody you love … it leaves you feeling empty. But I guess I'm not entirely empty. I still have my fighting instincts left." She squeezes my hand back. "I would like to meet your friend."

#

I expect it to be difficult to explain to Tonnie and John how I came across Althea, but it's easier. They believe the story I tell them—that I was going for a walk, seeking determination—even though the lie tastes sour. How do they not see straight through me?

We decide to have Althea meet us at the diner so I can introduce her to Tonnie and John. The lipstick stains were still embedded in the booth, now looking less like writing and more like blood. *It'll be okay, you're doing the right thing right now,* I remind myself, unable to calm down my dizzying nerves. John must notice because he asks me if I'm feeling all right.

After assuring and reassuring him several times that I'm fine, we sit down to talk to Althea. He and Tonnie shared their story, switching off when the story sometimes became hard to tell. Althea also told her story, which John verified through research before they even met with her. I'm lucky they didn't investigate me or else I definitely wouldn't be at this table. When they eventually moved onto actual information regarding the church, they both became almost mechanical about the process. At one point, John even slowed down—noticing Althea's peaked face—to say, "Sorry. We've been going over all of this for years, so we know it top to bottom. I'll slow down." He did, and I could tell Althea was grateful. I'm sure her confusion is worsened because she's still mourning her husband.

Eventually, John slips a new paper from a manila file folder onto the table. "And take a look here. Ezra was arrested for theft. It was only on one account and his charge was only community service. To be honest, it's important information, but it's not useful. He was an adult, but still younger, and I'm afraid this could be summed up to immaturity. He stole a diamond from a woman he worked for and tried to pawn it. The woman was quoted as saying she liked him and probably wouldn't have charged him if the police weren't involved. Besides, he'd probably say he was taking the money to feed the homeless or save an animal rescue."

"So we're just going to do nothing?" Tonnie asks. "I'm not comfortable with that. I understand your point, but this is what we've been looking for and it's all we have."

"You're right, but it's not enough. It's too far back in his history and it doesn't have anything to do with the church. Using this would also alert him that we're looking into him. We want to keep this thing as under wraps as possible for as long as we can."

Except it's not under wraps … An ever-growing pit in my stomach deepens.

"What else can we do?" Althea asks. "I'm willing to do anything you need."

I hold up my hand. "I have an idea."

Beside me, John grins. He laces his hand through mine. "Go ahead."

"Well, I don't know if or how much we'll be able to find on Ezra, but I think we should also have a fallback plan. Even if we can't *stop* the church, we might be able to *end* it by ruining Ezra's reputation. Stories like yours matter, and if those stories come from you, people have to listen. I think we should try to find more people who were burned by the church and start some sort of group. A community of stories might be the push people need in order to believe the church is bad."

"You're exactly right, Kin," John says, his eyes glowing with excitement. "I don't know how I never thought about this before."

"I honestly didn't think about it until I met Althea."

"You're such a genius," he says, which earns me a kiss on the side of the head. "I've been thinking about all of this in a personal way, when I should've been widening my scope."

"I'm sure most people want to bring Ezra down just as much as we do," Tonnie adds.

"And those who want to remain anonymous can just write their account of what happened," Althea says.

"But how are we going to find these people?" Tonnie asks.

"That's where it might be harder," I say. "John has a list of everyone who's been 'healed' since he started going there, so I was thinking we could cross-reference that with social media and whatever else we can find. We look for people who passed or family members who show negative feelings toward the church."

"So we vet them first. Good plan," John agrees. "Talking to people should also give us an idea of their standing. Maybe I'll compile the list and we can each work on our own sections?"

"That sounds good to me," Althea says. "Maybe I can … work on it here? Going home, unless it's to eat or sleep, feels a little unbearable right now."

"Yes, please. That's perfectly fine," Tonnie tells her, laying her hand over Althea's like a concerned friend. "Those things take time."

"Thank you," Althea says. "Thank all of you. I don't know what I would've done if I hadn't met Kinley and she hadn't introduced me to you."

I only smile at Althea, wishing I could tell her the same thing. I was going to break into Ezra's files, but that wouldn't have gotten me anywhere compared to what we're doing now. Before, I was just patching up the problems I created, but now I'm contributing an actual solution.

#

John's list is longer than I expect. Maybe he's been attending the church longer than any of us knew. The only reason why Ezra noticed him in the first place was because one of the congregates complained that he elbowed her repeatedly during the service while he was writing. She was obviously trying to stir up trouble. Now that I know John, I wonder if he maybe only elbowed her once, then she built it up to sound like a nine-round boxing match.

I mentally cross out some of the names on the list, because I already know they're loyal to Ezra or paid plants. He always has the plants sign to say they won't release any information, and I usually end up as the one filing it. I can't tell John about them, of course, so our research takes longer, since we have to go through these people.

Luckily, John does the research while I make notes. I'm glad, because I don't have a lot of experience with technology until recently, other than my cellphone.

John's sitting over at his desk, while I'm at his dining table with a pad of paper and organizing the documents he's printed. We took a break to take Clancy for a half-hour walk, and she's been staring at me ever since. I swear she's fond of me, but she still acts extremely judgmental—I'm sure her intuition is telling her I'm not who I say I am.

"This Caleb Rooker seems like a lead," John says slowly, still reading. "Maybe put him on the list to follow up with. Ezra actually 'healed' him and, according to social media, he's in remission. I thought maybe he might've just been playing it up, except he's not thanking the church *at all*."

"That's suspicious," I agree. "Clearly he doesn't think Ezra had anything to do with it or else he'd be singing his praises."

"We'll feel him out then," he says.

"By any chance, do you know anything about the history of the church?" I ask John, trying to lead him in another direction.

"I know what's out there. Ezra took over the church after their previous pastor retired. Do you think I should look into it further?"

"Maybe. You never know what you might find that could help." Meaning, he *will* find something.

Ezra didn't buy the church and suddenly gain a congregation. Truthfully, he stole it. After Ezra decided he wanted to try his hand at swindling on a new level, so he fudged his resume and applied for an associate pastor position at the Chestnut Pines Church, now the Church of Life. Instead of using the position as a way to learn, he started incorporating healings and asking for donations in his preaching. More than anything, we started catering to the parishioners with power. I don't remember what the church was like then, but as he slowly changed it into what it is today, he gained the majority he needed to force the original pastor into retirement. I can still remember the man coming over to our house the night of the board's vote, yelling at Ezra and calling him a scam artist. *You may not really believe in Him*, he'd said, *but He sees.*

As always, Ezra usually hid me away when people were around, but I'd snuck out when I'd heard the yelling. From the top of the stairs, with my face squeezed between the spindles, I watched the first and only time I would ever see Ezra get his just deserts. Nothing the pastor said was going to change anything, but it all still meant something.

All I can hope is the pastor would be willing to speak up. Who knows, he might even know some parishioners who left with him and would be willing to speak.

"If you'd been helping us from the very beginning, I doubt it would have taken us this long," John says, standing up. He stretches his arms out, then pops his neck from side to side. Something so simple should not make my heart do massive flips. But goodness, one look at him and all rational thought goes by the wayside. He's instant amnesia for the soul. "Why're you lookin' at me like that, Kin?"

My heart stutters, as it always does when he calls me that. I love that he's picked up the habit. It's like he's personalized my name and made it more special. It's something that belongs to the two of us now.

"I just ..." I blush. I've spent my whole life worrying I'm not enough—not smart enough, not pretty enough, not devious enough. This is the first time in my life I've wished I could be just one of those. Anything to help me handle the situation. "You can be a little distracting sometimes."

He cocks his head, obviously pretending he has no idea what I'm saying. "How so?"

"Having this conversation is going to ruin me."

"Don't be embarrassed," he says, walking toward me. His perfect, shiny teeth flash in a delicious, mischievous way. "It's hard to pay attention when you're around, too. It's that mixture of the smart and pretty ingredients you have going on."

A small, not-so-smart-or-pretty snort escapes from me. "Ingredients?"

"Are you trying to make me feel embarrassed now?" he says, right next to me. He leans one arm on the table and lays the other on the back of my chair, caging me in. "You can't just tell me I'm brilliant and handsome? It's only fair."

"You're very brill—"

I'm not sure which one of us moves first—I honestly think it's me—but suddenly we're kissing. He pulls me into him by looping his fingers through the belt loops on my jeans, then starts walking us backward. I follow, arching my back to deepen the kiss. Half the time I can't walk and chew gum at the same time, but walking and kissing John at the same time? Effortless.

But then that effortlessness is ruined when he trips backward over the threshold of his bedroom. I can't help but giggle when he bursts out laughing. The playing field is officially leveled. I've never felt so happy for an imperfection in my life. I don't feel so different—instead, I feel connected. To *him*.

"Damn, that hurt," he says, lifting his bare foot to rub at it.

He's what I've been dreaming of my entire life. Between his boyish smile and his compassionate brown eyes, I know this man's heart and soul are in the right place. He's always been who he says he is, even when he had no reason to trust me.

I wish I could do that for him. Someday, I hope I can. Until then, I can let him see parts of me no one else has seen. Not just the physical parts, but the broken, psychological ones.

While he's still frowning at his foot, I walk toward him. All his attention switches to me when I slide my hands up and over his chest, resting my arms on his shoulder. My lips meet his for a long, breathless kiss that reminds me of waves crashing against a shore then receding, then crashing again.

He takes another step back to sit on the bed, pulling me down with him. In an instant he has me beneath him, his leg between mine and our hearts hammering in tempo together.

Before long, we've lost our shirts and his lips have moved down my neck. When he dances his fingers over my nipple through my bra, my pelvis jolts against his thigh. I tangle my fingers in his hair, searching for something to do to help him along. He stops, though, to look up at me. "Keep going or stop?" he asks.

"Keep going," I whisper. *I'll combust if you don't.*

He smiles, reaching beneath me to undo the clasp of my boring white bra. He slips the straps down my arm as if he's uncovering a long-forgotten Egyptian Pharaoh's tomb. *Treasure. The Holy Grail. The meaning of everything.*

Right before he slips it off completely, he looks up at me and pauses. "That's a new expression. Care to explain it?"

"Not right now," I say.

He raises an eyebrow, then starts to push my strap back up.

"Fine." I laugh, which is really just a husky breath. "I feel special. I've never felt special before."

"Well, you should. Always." He moves up to kiss me, this time quick and reassuring. "You are to me, you know."

I don't know what to say. Luckily, I don't have to come up with anything, because he takes my bra off the rest of the way and stares down at my breasts with a hooded expression. I can't help but notice he's gone from hard to throbbing against my leg.

He gently—reverently—frames his hand over my damaged breast, rubbing his thumb over my nipple. It rises, begging for his touch. Then, to my amazement, he drops his head and takes it in his mouth. His tongue flicks and his teeth prod. My whole body starts to ache for more, wanting and needing this and that and everything else.

But I know that as bad as it is for me, it's just as bad for him, too. I don't want to be the only one feeling delicious. Tentatively, I run my hand down his abs and toward the hem of his jeans. He freezes when I start to undo the button there.

"Kinley," he chokes. "What are you doing?"

"I want you to feel as good as I do."

"Trust me, I feel pretty damn high on you," he says. "But only if you're sure."

"I am," I promise. He helps me take his jeans off, which are thrown somewhere with our shirts and my bra. He remains in his underwear, which is enough. I slip my hand beneath the band, taking his length in my hand.

When he jerks slightly, I realize I can judge my movements based on his moans, groans, and fervor.

But just as I'm getting comfortable with touching him, he slips his fingers to undo my jeans, then further until his fingers are inside them and beneath my underwear. He hooks his fingers inside of me and I cry out, losing all thought.

I can barely breathe when his lips meet mine again, our hands and fingers working each other over until finally something snaps inside of me like a flag in the wind. My whole body goes to tense and relaxed at the same time, bright lights blinding me. It's all I can do but arch into him, taking everything I can steal.

The euphoria fades slowly, and then John's gone— muffled groans come from the bathroom. When he comes out, he gives me an almost shy grin and then lays down on the bed beside me. He pulls my back against his chest, his arm over my breasts, then nestles his head in my hair.

"You are the most beautiful person I've ever met, Kinley," he whispers. "I'll be damned if I don't prove it to you."

CHAPTER 13

John

After a week, Kinley and I have a working list of people we want to contact. It's longer than I expected. Then again, we only might end up with a small handful of people who are willing to talk. Most people won't want to go against Ezra. Kinley and I assign ourselves a majority of the list to visit, since we'll be doing it together, then split the rest amongst Althea and Tonnie.

We're all going to try to contact people through social media first, then try to find another way if that doesn't work out. Luckily, Althea's got a human resource background, so she was able to craft a form letter that is more likely to make people willing to talk rather than scare them off. There's a fine line where you want them to know what we're about, but if we're too forward and also wrong about their allegiance, we're screwed.

After Kinley and I send all the messages we're supposed to (thankfully all were on social media except for two, but both had business emails), I lean back in my chair and let out a long sigh.

"I guess we wait now," Kinley says, matching my sigh.

She pulled up a dining room chair beside me.

"Seems that way. Hopefully somebody puts us out of our misery pretty soon." I leave the browser I'm in and pull up my email. There's an email there from a Gregory Harding that came in late last night. Turns out Kinley was onto something about looking into the origin of the church. Not that I'm surprised, since Kinley has a knack for intuition. I found Gregory Harding's name through a newspaper op-ed written back when Ezra first took over the church. One of his parishioners was trying to bring to light the underhandedness of Ezra Abel. He didn't have the proof to back it up so it didn't go anywhere. But there was one piece of evidence: a statement from Pastor Gregory Harding claiming he'd been forced out of the church. I wanted to contact the author of the piece, but it turns out she passed away a few years ago from an aneurysm. Gregory Harding is alive and well at the age of sixty-five, living three hours away and very willing to meet. "Here's the times Gregory can meet. I think Monday would be good since I'm off that evening. Maybe we can grab a hotel somewhere."

Kinley nods. "That works for me."

"Good, I'll let him know," I say and send back a quick email. "These are starting to feel like important pieces. The cogs are finally starting to turn, thanks to you."

"No, it's thanks to you," she says. "Without you, none of this would even be happening."

"You definitely have a way of making me feel better about myself," I tell her with a wink.

She blushes because she's a blusher no matter how much we kiss and where. And we've been doing that every spare minute we have, almost using it as a way to recharge our batteries after all the research. Even with so much progress, my main focus has been her. I never thought I could get distracted so easily or that something like this was in the cards for me.

She pats her knees, whistling for Clancy, who

immediately comes running from the bedroom and places her head in the gap between Kinley's knees. She rubs at Clancy's head, paying extra attention to her nose and her soft ears.

I don't know what this is with Kinley, but I know it's definitely coming on strong. There's so much in life I've missed out, mostly because I've been too afraid to go out and chase it. When you lose your family and have liars for enemies, it's hard to want to live life. You don't think you're ever capable of having anything normal. You want to steel your heart away and brace for the impending damage you're always expecting. But with Kinley, I feel at peace. A place where I can finally breathe and trust and just ... be.

Except there's still so much between us. Things unanswered from her I can't move forward without knowing. But I haven't really asked. Sure, I've tried once or twice, but I never prodded any further. Maybe she's just one of those girls that don't like to talk about themselves.

"I was thinkin'," I say, scratching at my chin. "I don't know your last name."

"Oh," she says, hands stilling on Clancy. "It's McKinley."

I raise an eyebrow. "Kinley McKinley?"

"No, Kathleen McKinley. My parents called me Katie." Her voice wavers as she talks about her parents, but she quickly seems to shoo the emotion away and gathers her strength back by going into something I can only call her story-mode. She turns off and a recording takes over in her place—as if she's telling me something she's repeated often and doesn't have to think about. Doesn't *want* to think about. "There was always at least three other Katies in any given care center and most families already had a Katie. So the social workers took to calling me Kinley instead. I liked the name because it was the one thing I had left of my mom and dad, other than my sister."

"I want to meet your sister sometime."

Kinley doesn't look at me and pets Clancy instead, who growls appreciatively, like a cat purring. "I don't think I want you to meet her yet, if that's okay."

I swallow, because damn, I didn't think she'd say that. It burns me a bit. "I understand."

"No, you don't," she says, turning toward me. She reaches out and grabs for my hand. "My sister—she's not like me. The way we were brought up sort of ruined her. I love her, but I'm not … I guess I'm embarrassed of her."

"You shouldn't be," I say, squeezing her hand. I press a kiss against her lips, then lean back. "We can't choose our family, but we're stuck with them anyway. But I'm happy to wait to meet her."

"Thank you." She pushes her hair behind her ear. "I promise it has nothing to do with you."

"I get it, Kin."

She points at the computer, standing up. "Somebody got back to us already."

"Wow, quick to the draw," I say.

We both lean forward, reading the message from a Lara Mallory.

John, yes, I used to attend the Church of Life. Ezra Abel trusted me as a follower and asked if I would be willing to be healed, but not disclose any information to anyone. At the time, I had just been diagnosed with ovarian cancer. I thought Ezra had to have a gift if he knew I needed to be healed. I thought all my prayers had been answered. But then the day of the healing came and his daughter took me back to the bathroom in the middle of the healing, then put something on a napkin—something supposed to look like a tumor. I was so shocked that it was all fake and so heartbroken because I wouldn't be getting healed, I just went along with everything.

In your email, you said you only wanted to know why I left the church. Maybe I'm reading between the lines, but I feel like you're trying to do something—maybe trying to close the Church of Life? It might just be false hope. But regardless, Ezra Abel is a liar and he's cheating everyone in his congregation. Please let me know if you want to meet and if there's anything I can do.

I'm sure my eyes are larger than pizzas when I look over at Kinley. A piece of me wants to jump up, throw my hands in the air, and do some sort of a crazy jig. I've been fueled by nervous energy for the last few days, but now it's all cumulated into something far more powerful. I feel almost as if I've been released from a cage—I'm suddenly rambunctious.

Kinley grins at me. It's the widest, brightest smile I've ever seen from her. "We're getting somewhere," she says.

The word comes from her lips as a gasp for air, "*Finally.*" I look up toward the ceiling—toward a real God or whoever's up there—thinking of my dad, my mom, Velma, and everyone else who deserves compensation.

\#

By about halfway through the week, Kinley and I have met with about ten people, each with a different story. Two of them were clearly still brainwashed by Ezra but had left because family had forced them to. Kinley thought maybe we should reach out to their family members instead. The other ones were exactly what we've been looking for, some with stories like Lara, others who could see through the church. Each story is a piece to a puzzle that had been previously filled with gaping holes.

Tonnie and Althea haven't had as many successes, but they've still made progress. At this point, we count everything as a win because it's all more than we expected.

We record all of our conversations, with the person's permission, of course. Best case scenario, it's something we can take to a police officer or a lawyer. Worst case—which isn't bad, either—we make a web page to spread the word. No matter what, I have this vision of Ezra standing in front of a church with no people in it. Instead of him, people will turn to doctors or counselors or authentic people in touch with religion—everyone who can really *help.*

Even with my dad, some sort of family counseling or maybe a talk about the afterlife might've been enough to leave us with some sort of a resolution. Instead, all we had to cling to was Ezra's false word.

For the first time in days, I'm on my own. Kinley had to go into work.

Another thing that's starting to play on my mind—how is it I work five days a week but Kinley's almost always free? I don't want to question it. I refuse to go throwing things away when the good outweighs the bad by a landslide. I just can't help wondering what she's holding back. Maybe there's something embarrassing she doesn't want me to know or she's afraid she'll scare me off. And even if her job isn't what she's told me—of if she doesn't have one at all—I think I could accept that, too.

When will she finally *completely* trust me? Given the feelings I already have for her, I'm willing to wait.

Even though I'm deep in thought, I'm not surprised when Clancy starts barking on our walk and I glance up to see Prudence standing there. Her arms are crossed, hair pulled back in a tight bun, a pale pink peacoat on. One of her booted toes is tapping, as if she's pissed I'm not on schedule to walking my dog.

The more and more I see her, the uglier she gets. Sure, she's pretty, but that ruthless, cold part of her makes her something of a nightmare. I'll bet if she didn't have Ezra for a father, she'd still be playing the same type of game. She thrives on this lifestyle.

I don't even stop, pulling Clancy past her and heading toward the patch of woods where we usually walk. The taps of Prudence's footsteps follow behind me, gaining speed until she's beside me.

"That was a nasty thing you did," I tell her.

Out of the corner of my eye, I see her shrug. "That's your opinion."

"I'm sure it would've been the police's opinion, too."

"You didn't call the police."

"That was Tonnie's decision," I clarify. I'm careful to keep my voice even—emotionless. "If it was up to me, I'd have called them. You vandalized her diner."

"And said something mean about your lady love. Let's be honest, *that's* what you're angry about."

"I'm pissed over everything."

"I say it's all very unfair," she says, her voice loud and theatric. Clancy growls for real, which makes Prudence pause. Only for a breath, though. "All I was trying to do was pull the wool out from over your eyes."

"Clearly, you're putting my best interest first," I say, sarcastically.

We finally make it to the tree line and I stop. Clancy makes no move to explore the area. She stays next to me, tail down and dark gaze glued to Prudence. Mine is, too. "You realize if that were the case, you would've have vandalized property. Permanently, by the way. Some of the words are still pretty visible."

She grins. Cheshire cat eat your heart out. "Which words?"

"Words I'm not willing to say in front of a seventeen-year-old kid," I say.

"Ouch," she says, her grin just barely faltering. "I was only trying to be honest, you know. Little Kinley isn't what you think she is."

"And you know that how?"

She leans down to Clancy, patting her head. Clancy rears away, showing her teeth. Prudence only groans. "Let's just keep it at *I know things*."

I smile, hoping it's dripping with deprecation. "Here's the thing: you'll do and say just about anything to get your way. Your word isn't good enough for me."

"Oh, so you would believe me if there were proof?" She slips her hands to her hips, standing taller. "The trust doesn't run as deep as you want everyone to believe, does it? There are some things that don't"— she steps closer, tapping a finger against my chest; I don't dare touch her to move her way because who knows how she'd spin that—"add up."

"What is the point of all of this, Prudence?" I ask. "I agreed to stay quiet about the church. What else is it you want?"

"Honesty," she says in an outburst. "Out of everyone, I'm the one who *should* be the easiest to trust. I am *not* a liar."

Her tone takes me off guard. Sure, she's been immature this entire time—even when she's trying to pretend to be worldly—but this is an entirely new level. She's like an insecure kid. No matter how much I might not believe her, she completely believes in what she's saying.

"If people would be honest, then there wouldn't be any issues," she continues. "Maybe my way of purging the truth wasn't the right way—not that I'm admitting anything—but at least it was the truth. If you would just open your eyes, you might realize that. But you and everyone else are just so wrapped up in Ezra Abel."

"And you aren't?"

"No."

"Then why are you doing his bidding?"

"Because there's a difference between believing in someone and doing what they want. Only one of those gets me the things *I* want."

"And what is it you think you're getting from Ezra?"

"Look at you pumping me for information. Are you recording this?"

"I didn't exactly come prepared to be shanghaied while walking my dog."

As if agreeing, Clancy sits down with yet another growl. Prudence tilts her head, sizing her up. "Are you ever in a good mood?" she asks my dog. She sighs and looks to me. "Ezra is my guardian, so I don't have a choice but to live with him. But I also have room to network and skills to gain. Plus, he has to die eventually, and there's no way he'll leave that church to Michelle. She's lucky if she even knows what day it is."

"The Board decides who leads the church."

She waves a hand. "Not really."

"All right then. How about the fact that Ezra's only twenty years older than you? He's not going to be decrepit and ready for the home anytime soon."

"I came here to rain on your parade, not for you to rain on mine," she says with a pout.

"I think it's time for you to leave."

She ignores me. "Are you coming to church this week?"

"I don't think so," I say, walking away. Clancy is more than willing to go with me and get away from Prudence. I doubt Prudence will follow and risk getting her shoes muddy now that the snow has melted.

"Darn, and I had something planned. Next time then. It can wait. I'll taste better with time anyway."

With that, she walks away. I can't help thinking I'm happy I'll be missing whatever it is happening in her messed up, devious little mind.

LIZ ASHLEE

CHAPTER 14

Kinley

I purposefully left John with the excuse of having to work, knowing I'd be able to catch Michelle home alone. Ezra is scheduled for a book club meeting at one of the rich parishioner's homes. I'm pretty sure "book club" is code for "card game." Ezra always comes home with extra money in his pocket and the stench of alcohol on his clothes. I'm not sure why he goes through the trouble of lying, other than maybe he doesn't want other parishioners to know.

I think Ezra spends so much time pretending to be righteous, he uses that as a dubious outlet. It's just funny he seems to think gambling is the worst of all the things he does.

Michelle is spending her night free of Ezra knitting. I remember her doing that a lot when I was a little girl. She also played the piano—it wasn't church tunes then, but songs that could either make your heart happy or make you want to cry. She was never much of a mother, but she was the only semblance of one I had.

She's working on a purple scarf, with pink and blue

ones already finished, and sitting on the end table beside the couch.

This is also one of the few nights she can be found without a bottle of wine or her bottle of pills. I want to talk to the real Michelle, not the half-here version. Similar to the pastor Ezra pushed out, Michelle feels like a missing link I can use. Except I don't really know how to bridge that subject.

"Oh, Kinley," she says, setting her knitting down. "I didn't know you were home. You've been gone a lot, lately."

I'm surprised she's even noticed that. "I've been spending a lot of time with John."

"Hmm," she says, then turns the scarf she's working on over in her hands. "So Prudence was right that you have feelings for him?"

I nod, then realize she's not looking at me to see. "Yes."

"Maybe it's time you leave."

She says it so simply it takes me a while to actually process her words. By the time I have, she's back to knitting, almost as if she didn't say anything. Her hands are shaking, something I've never noticed before. It could be that she's going without her usual substances, but it feels like more. I'm so used to her care-free personality—as though she's floating above us, watching us. Here, lately, it's seemed as if she's trying to do more and actually interact with me. I can't help thinking she's trying to say something without really saying it.

I take a seat on the recliner catty-cornered to her. "Do you ever wish you could leave, Michelle?"

She doesn't stop knitting. "No."

"But you wish I would?"

"Yes."

"Do you see what he's doing to you?"

"Yes," she says. A faint, sad smile touches her lips. "Just as much as I see I'm doing it to myself."

"But what if you could escape that?"

"I can't," she says.

"Maybe you can. Maybe you drink and take the pills Ezra tells you to because that's your way of escaping."

She sets down her knitting and looks at me, more sober than I've ever seen her. "Kinley, those are the only things I *can* do to escape. I used to love our lifestyle, and then I realized how wrong it all is …. Now I'm paying for all that we took."

"That's Ezra's nonsense."

She shakes her head. "I tried to leave him, but my parents wouldn't support me. They called him and he forced me back into his life. Then we adopted you and your sister and I definitely couldn't leave you two with him. Now you're older and it's no use. I'm complicit in everything he's done."

"I think if you admitted …"

"Stop there," she commands quietly. "Whatever you're doing, I won't tell Ezra, but I refuse to be involved. I want you to find happiness and safety away from Ezra and Prudence, even me. We're all thorns waiting to be pricked." Michelle moves her fingers over the scarf, pulling it to loosen the knitting. Her eyes fall to the clock, as if she's counting down the minutes until Ezra comes home. When she's satisfied, she looks back to me. "I wish I could have given you a better life."

"You did, Michelle."

"No, I didn't." She looks off into the distance, gaze far away. "I grew up with two parents who loved each other, three sisters, one brother, and a brick house with not enough bathrooms. I thought that life needed to be more … but it's not more than that. There was *love* in that house, and you girls have only been raised in indifference. Look what it did to Prudence and look what it's doing to you."

"I'm going to make it better—for all of us."

"I hope you do, but I don't think you will."

She sets down her knitting, stands to stretch her legs

and back, then heads off in the direction of the bathroom, probably for self-medication. I know she could be the most powerful of allies against Ezra, but she doesn't want to be. I think Ezra's pushed Michelle into a hopeless, helpless corner where she can't be reached.

Whatever I do, I can't let him do the same for me. If given the choice, I have to put myself first above everyone else—including Prudence—if I want to come out of this whole.

#

Althea invites John and me over to dinner the following evening. When we get there, she wraps us both in hugs and tells us that this is our thank you dinner for giving her purpose following her husband's death. Before she goes back to setting the table, she takes us on a tearful tour of all of her pictures with him.

The cute, yellow bungalow reminds me of something out of a realtor magazine, with a sense of style and hominess that makes you wonder if the place has a beating heart in its walls. When Michelle was talking earlier, is this the type of home she was talking about growing up in?

John leans into me while Althea gets busy with the chicken and artichoke rice casserole she promised will "change our lives." He presses his hand into my back and places a light kiss at my ear. "I'm never sure what to do with all the crying," he whispers.

"I don't know either," I whisper back.

"Bad thing, because I'm usually the crier," he says with a wink.

I can't tell if he's being serious or not, but I have a suspicion he is. I love that he *shows* his emotions. Everyone else I know either hides theirs or plays them to an extreme.

"You two are honestly the cutest couple I've met," Althea says, setting plates down with a *clank*. "Come, come," she demands pleasantly. "Time to eat."

"I, uh, brought over some wine," John tells her, holding up the bottle we stopped on the way here for. "I hope you like dry."

"I don't, but I drink it anyway." She makes a spinning motion finger by her ear. "The sweet stuff goes to my head pretty fast. Neither of you want that on your hands. The glasses are in that cabinet if you want to get them down and pour us a bowl—er, glass."

She gives us both a playful grin, then goes back to setting the table. John mimics her finger twirl before he goes off to do wine duty.

"Thank you so much for inviting us, Althea," I say, walking toward her.

"It's the least I can do." She waves me off. "Honestly, I haven't felt this hopeful and energized in *years*. I only wish my husband were still alive to witness what we're doing. But he's somewhere watching." Tears start to form at the corner of her eyes, but she wipes at them. "This is not boding well for my tough exterior, is it?"

"I don't think being sad counts against you," I tell her. "We're all allowed to be sad."

"Well, give me time and you'll get to know the real Althea. Let me tell you. I am a badass."

John snorts. "You know, I am not surprised to hear that."

"I just need to get my confidence and my energy back," Althea says. "As I'm sure you understand more than anyone, John."

I can't help but notice John pours their glasses of wine a little fuller. Althea puts a large spoonful of casserole on each of our plates, along with two breadsticks. We all sit down and she immediately breaks one of the breadsticks in half and dips it as if the casserole is a sauce.

As soon as I've swallowed a forkful and my taste buds are exposed to absolute heaven, I nudge John with my knee. I can reach him because Althea has a small, round table that looks like something you'd find in a cafe.

"I think Tonnie might have competition," I say to him.

He groans. "I know, and I hate it. Althea, I'm going to disown Tonnie and adopt you as my step-aunt-whatever."

"Please don't," Althea says, pointing her fork at him. "Badass or not, I don't think I'd win in a fight against her."

"She is wily," John agrees.

We eat in silence for a few minutes before Althea takes a sip of her wine and sets it down with an inquisitive look on her face. "Now, Kinley, I don't think I know why you're involved in all of this. What are your stakes?"

I take my time chewing on a piece of chicken before I answer her so I can craft my words. "I just really care for John and I want to help him find peace."

"That's very sweet of you, Kinley," Althea says. "John's lucky he has you."

John grins before popping bread in his mouth, chewing, then saying, "I'm the luckiest man alive, that's for damn sure."

Martyr-sized guilt cements in the pit of my stomach. "It's hard not to want to help. I'm sure anyone in my position would do whatever they could, too."

"I would hope so," Althea says. "But people also like to hide away from the truth and do whatever's easiest. I don't know if I would've gotten involved if I hadn't stepped foot in that church." She reaches forward and takes a big sip of wine. "But I really don't want to talk about the church right now. No, I want to know what's in the cards for the two of you when all of this is over."

John coughs, his neck reddening. *Is he nervous?* "Well, Kinley and I haven't been together long enough to …"

"Somebody's got his mind in a jewelry store, hasn't he?" Althea says, making a clucking noise with her tongue. "No, I mean separately. What do you want to do? Hobby or job or dream?"

John chuckles, clearly relieved. On my end, I can't find the confidence to do much of anything. Is John that far ahead? I want to be, but I just can't let my mind go there.

Whenever I think about a future with him, I see myself walking down an aisle on Ezra's arm, John's face filled with hatred for the both of us as he realizes …

John's suddenly passionate tone pulls me out of my personal nightmare. "I've thought about this a lot lately. I don't think I can begin to name the things I want to do. I want to write a non-fiction book—I enjoy investigating and I'd like to do it more long-term, but on something I'm not as close to. I also want to talk to my station manager about switching to days and work on trying to exist amongst the living. I also want to try traveling—I've never really gone on a vacation before. I haven't even left the state, which is ridiculous when you think about it."

"It's not ridiculous," Althea says. "You've been busy. I'll tell you now, though, there aren't many places better than where we are right now. We get to experience all the seasons, we're a stone's throw away from the beach, but also close to the mountains. There's no vacation better than living here. What about you, Kinley?"

"Oh, I don't know," I say. I push around the food on my plate with my fork. "I want to learn more about my biological parents. I don't know very much about them or their history."

"I didn't realize you were adopted," Althea says.

"My sister and I are orphans," I tell her.

"Sweetheart, how terrible." She reaches out to squeeze my free hand. "Were you young?"

John answers for me. "She was."

"I can't imagine. Do you remember much about them?"

"Not very much," I admit. "Things here and there. Sometimes memories will come back to me. My sister's not as lucky."

"Well, then, I think connecting with the past will be good for you," she says. "It'll help you know yourself better."

"And, of course, I'd be happy to help you," John tells

me.

"Just as long as I'm not your next research project," I say with a laugh. "So what about you, Althea?"

"I'm not sure. I'm having to re-evaluate everything I ever dreamed of. I had dreams separate of my husband, obviously, but he was always supposed to be with me when they came true. Before he got sick, we talked about trying for a baby. I know it's unconventional as a single parent, but I think I would love to look into adoption. If I'm ever ready to remarry, I doubt I'll be able to have children at that point in time."

"I think that would be good for you," I tell her. "I'm sure you would be a wonderful mom."

"I would hope so. What are your adoptive parents like?"

"You're going for the hard-hitting questions, aren't you?" John jokes.

"Sorry, it's the marketing person inside. I have to act like a reporter before I can spin a story or gain interest."

"It's fine," I tell her. "My adoptive parents aren't the best. I like my … adoptive mom, although she's not much of a mom really. But her husband—I don't like him. They only fostered us originally for the money."

"I hate hearing that. Why did they adopt you then?" she asks.

"It looked better that way," I admit. "They care about those sorts of things."

"They're religious," John explains.

If you only knew. "But I can't be too mad because they kept my sister and me together." Perhaps the only good thing I've witnessed Ezra do.

"That is one blessing," Althea agrees. "Now, while I go get our desert ready, think about how you're going to tell me the story of how the two of you first met."

#

"Thanks to Althea," John says on our drive back to his place, "I don't think I have any more secrets to spill or room for food left."

"She's definitely good at what she does," I agree.

"And I think she's taken by you," he says. "If you weren't an adult, I think she'd adopt you, previous adoption be damned."

"I like her a lot," I admit. "It's nice to have someone who wants to mother me a little bit."

"A little bit? I've never been read the riot act like that before," he tells me.

After maybe a glass too many of the wine, Althea went on a modest rant pointed at John on how he *has* to treat me as the strong, independent queen I am. *If you ruin this, I'll dig you a grave so deep Hades will be your next-door neighbor,* were her exact word. We both believed her.

"Okay, so maybe you should be worried for your life if you take a misstep," I tell him.

"That sounds more like it," he confirms. "But I really think she's good for you. Between her and Tonnie—"

"And you," I add.

He chuckles, the sound embracing me in the dark car. "And me, you're different than the first time I met you. Well, not a different person, but changed. You've come into yourself."

"I just didn't have very much before."

"Yeah, and you deserve better than that."

I can't help but reach for his hand to press my lips against his knuckles. He has so much confidence in me. More than I'll ever hope to have.

He swallows, suddenly uneasy. "Prudence came by again yesterday."

My head rears so sharply my neck pops. "She did?" When is she going to listen to me?

"Yeah. She was spouting her usual nonsense. I talked to her, hoping it would satisfy her. At this point, I don't know what'll do that. Something short of a miracle, I'd say."

"I thought maybe she was finally getting the message."

"I hoped so, but she's got a message she wants me to get, too."

"What's that?"

"I don't know, really. She keeps going on about liars. She sounds pretty paranoid, even calling you one. Personally, I'd say she's grasping at straws, but she's so serious and clearly believes everything she's saying."

"She called me a liar?" Oh God, what if she's gearing up to tell him the truth? And there's nothing I can do about it. Even if it comes from me, he'll still hate me.

"She's the liar. Not you," he says.

"John, I'm not a saint, either."

"I know," he says. "But no matter what, you're better than the things she has to say."

I let go of his hand to nervously run my fingers through the ends of my hair. "There are things you don't know about me ..."

"I've prepared myself for that already," he admits. He glances over at me as we pull into his usual spot at the back of his apartment. "Whatever it is, I'm willing to wait for you to tell me and accept anything you have to say."

"No matter what?"

"No matter what," he confirms.

He sounds so sure, and when he looks at me, his expression is confident also. Furrowed brow, tightened jaw, clear eyes. I almost believe him. Maybe I've been underestimating him this entire time. I might just be doing an injustice to the both of us. I mean, it has to count for something if I'm willingly trying to help. At the end of the day, I've chosen him above everyone and everything else.

I lean across the space between us to kiss him, taking charge. Tongue and lips and teeth engage in a battle completely unlike the way John and I are normally. We're fighting to get as close to each other as we can. He grins, pressing his hand against my neck. "How about we wait until we're inside?"

I nod, breathing a little heavy. We both slip out of the car and then he takes me by the hand, tugging me toward his apartment. If Clancy barks, neither of us pays any attention. We'll take her for a walk later. Right now, all we can see, hear, feel is each other.

He leads me back toward his bedroom, where we immediately take off our clothes—all except my underwear. We've gotten farther, but not beyond this point. As much as my body is screaming at me to take this to the next level, I can't. I need to wait until I'm sure of my feelings. I don't want to put either of us through the wringer of my soul-searching journey.

I curl my hands into his hair as his lips travel down neck, breasts, and abdomen, settling at the space just above my underwear. He pulls at it with his teeth, then grins up at me.

I nod, digging my fingers into the rumpled sheets. He pulls my underwear down slowly until I'm completely bare in front of him. He stares at me, eyes glowing in the moonlight room, before he ducks his head. His tongue flicks out against my heat, causing me to gasp and my hips to buckle. I'm not sure if I say his name out loud or in my mind, but it's the only thing I have room to think about.

John.

His tongue works me, fingers adding extra pressure. "You're amazing, Kin," he says, sound waves rumbling. My heart feels as though it's gone into quarter notes, rearing up toward heaven.

When his thumb and tongue both hit a specific spot, my whole body bows and tenses. Bright lights and sparkles fill my sight, something like waves crashing against the shores in my ears. Heaven on earth.

CHAPTER 15

John

Tonnie looks me over when I walk into the diner to give her the keys to my apartment so she can let Clancy out while Kinley and I are away. I caught her in the middle of cleaning dishes in the kitchen, so she has water splashes all over her.

"What's on your mind?" I ask suspiciously as I hand her the keys.

She puts them in the pocket of her apron, then shrugs noncommittally.

"It's not like you to *not* say what you're thinking."

"I was just thinking that you actually look awake."

I give her a confused look. "Because I'm normally asleep?"

"Normally you look dead-tired, given you sleep less than a cat spends awake. But you also look healthier." She steps on her toes and pats my cheek a few times, leaving soap suds behind. "Color in your cheeks." Then she pinches my arm. More suds. "More skin on your bones."

I don't know where she's planning on going next, but I stop her there, then wipe at the suds. "I get the picture."

She laughs, going back to the dishes. "I'm just happy to see you looking healthier. You haven't been taking very good care of yourself and it's beginning to show."

"Great," I say. "I've been a billboard for dysfunction."

"Oh, don't overdramatize."

"You're the one making it sound like I'm on death's door."

She rolls her eyes. "So you'll be back tomorrow afternoon?"

"Yeah, we're leaving now, meeting with him this afternoon, then checking in at the hotel."

"Well, be careful and let me know how your meeting goes."

"I will definitely do that." I pull out my phone to check the time. "Kinley should be here in a minute."

"She's riding the bus?"

"Yeah."

"I wish she'd let you pick her up."

"I don't think she wants me to meet her parents, which is fine. Not everyone loves their family like I love you," I remind her.

She makes a harrumph noise. "You don't have to go *inside*."

"You know what? Let's go back to the part where you're happy I'm eating."

"No, I'm happy you're healthy. You ate just fine before. That was not the problem, and your tab knows it."

"How can I have tab when half the time I pay and the other half of the time you say it's on the house?"

"Because I like saying it. It's one of those perks of being a business owner."

"So you say it but you don't mean it?"

Her gesture, summed up in one word, is, *Duh*.

I frown. "Let me know how much I owe you then."

This time she just waves me off. "We'll keep the tab running until I need you to pay for my retirement."

"Ah, glad I know about that now rather than later." My

phone buzzes with a text from Kinley telling me she's here. I tell her I'll be out in a second, then lean down to kiss Tonnie on the cheek. "Love you."

"Love you, too, kid. Stay safe," she says. "And maybe have a little fun after your meeting. Just for a change?"

"Will do," I promise her.

I head back out into the eating area and grab my duffle bag from the corner by the entrance. Tonnie wasn't wrong about having some fun. After our meeting, I'm taking Kinley out to dinner, then to a park on a river. According to the Google search I did, the nightlife there is one of the number one attractions, even when it's cold out.

I'm hoping our meeting will go well and we'll be in the mood for it. Kinley and I haven't gotten a chance to do anything really special and I want us to have that. It's a taste of what might come after Ezra Abel and Church of Life. It's as much fuel to finish as much as it is some sort of a safety net.

She's sitting on the bus stop bench, waiting for me. Her hair is curled and it looks like she's wearing makeup, which isn't something I'm used to.

"You look real pretty right now," I tell her. "Not that you don't always."

"Thank you," she says. "Althea did my makeup for me. I wanted to look more professional when we meet with Gregory." She blushes, looking up at me through her lashes. "And for tonight."

All I can do is tug her gently by her hand and kiss her deeply. By the time we've finally come up for air, my arms are numb from my stronghold on the duffle. She has a small, brown backpack sitting on the bench that looks like something out of the seventies.

I pick it up and sling it over my shoulder to carry it. "It matches my eyes, doesn't it?" I ask.

She smiles, shaking her head. "I think you're going to start a trend, for sure."

#

Our drives goes by fast because I take it as an opportunity to catch Kinley up on all my favorite music. I'm surprised when there are a few she admits to not liking, although most she enjoys and wants to hear again. By the time we get off the highway and start taking backroads, she actually gets a few of the references I make. As we start to rely on GPS more, I turn down the music and our conversation takes a break.

Gregory lives near the church he preaches at part-time, but he doesn't say where and gives us directions to the church instead. I'm sure that makes him feel more comfortable. Most people we've met with have requested to meet in public places, rather than at their home, simply for the reason that any association with Ezra Abel probably seems sketchy to them. There's really no way to know if we're against him as we say we are. Most people can hopefully guess Kinley and I wouldn't be Ezra's chosen choice of muscle.

Gregory's church is an old, red-bricked building in what is the historic part of the town. Our drive in took us through a bustling portion with chain stores and restaurants. This part is where the city building, post office, and salon are. The word "Bank" is carved into the stone above the church's front doors, meaning the church is in a repurposed building.

"Is that him?" Kinley asks as we pull up to park at the curb.

"I think so."

There's a man sitting on a bench by the front doors, wearing a heavy, black coat with khaki pants. He's tan, with his dark gray hair and well-groomed beard and wrinkled skin at his forehead, eyes, and mouth. Without even knowing him, I can tell he probably laughs a lot. He's the type of person who you trust because he's not going to lead you in the wrong direction. The opposite of Ezra.

"John and Kinley?" he asks when we get out. His voice is deep and has a heavy twang.

"Yes," I say, then shake his hand. Kinley does the same. "Thanks for meeting with us."

He smiles broadly. "I've been praying for something like this for a while. Leaving that church took a toll on my conscience. Thank you for helping to clear it."

He leads us inside the church and into a small entrance room with a table in the middle, there are fake sunflowers on it and pamphlets about the church. There's a standing bulletin board with community news on it next to the table. He takes both my coat Kinley's and hangs them up with his own in the closet.

"We can talk in the conference room," he says, motioning toward a room to the side.

The conference room has large burgundy chairs with a coffee table in front. Judging from the opened box of tissues and the tart warmer, the room is meant to be more of a *counseling* room. The church we used for my parents' funeral had a room similar to this one, which is where Tonnie and I spent the half-hour before their services crying. I don't remember ever seeing anything like this at the Church of Life.

Kinley and I take chairs next to each other. Gregory sits across from us. Without his coat, it's clear he has a gigantic cross on display around his neck. With Kinley in her sweater dress and tights, and me in my slacks and button-down, I can't help feeling as if we're doing some sort of a Catholic engagement tradition. Somehow, that would make me less nervous.

I lean forward on my knees, then straighten back up. I don't want to be rude. I settle for setting my arms on the armrests. "Is it okay if I record our conversation?" I ask, getting my phone out. "I won't use it without your permission, but I'd just like to have it for my own notes and records."

Gregory nods. "That sounds fair. How many people

have you already spoken with?"

"We've met with nine so far, though we've got ten scheduled for the next few weeks and several people we haven't heard back from."

"Color me surprised," Gregory says. "I didn't realize there'd be that many willing to speak out."

"There's more. Those numbers are Kinley and I's meetings, but my aunt and a friend have their own sets of people, too."

"Wow," he says, leaning back. He looks genuinely blown away. "You all have been working hard. Good for you."

"Thank you," I say. "It's been a long time coming."

"And how do you fit into all of this?" he asks, looking to Kinley. I'm not sure why she keeps getting asked that or why she suddenly gets shy about it.

She stutters something that isn't much of an answer, so I answer his question for her. "Kinley and I are together. When I told her about all of this, she offered to help. She's been wonderful."

"Oh, so you didn't know anything about the church before meeting John?" Gregory asks.

Kinley shakes her head. "No. No idea."

"Hmm," is all he says. "Where do you want me to start?"

"The beginning," I answer.

He raises his eyebrows but does as I've asked. He starts by telling me about how he came to the church, his hopes for it, then why he decided to hire an associate pastor. The backstory of a growing church which is genuinely doing good for the community clears up something that's been muddled up in my brain—I've been thinking of Ezra and the church as being one identity, but they're not. The church was swallowed up and poisoned by Ezra. Taking down the church and taking down Ezra don't need to be interchangeable. The church can continue to exist, so long as there's somebody leading it like Gregory—somebody who is honest in his profession.

As soon as Gregory moves toward talking about Ezra, his voice changes. It's laced with resentment, not just for himself but for those negatively affected or trapped by Ezra's lies.

"He managed to get the entire board to move in favor of firing me and making him head pastor. I didn't understand until one of the board members reached out to me shortly after Ezra started making the healings a main attraction of his circus. Evidently he'd found I'd been previously married and used that as a reason to plant doubt. It wasn't something I made a habit of telling people because we'd lost a child and our marriage didn't survive that. Ezra didn't know those details, so he made some up. What he said was very ugly against my character."

"I'm so sorry he did that to you," Kinley says quietly.

"At the time, it made me question my calling. But now I see that it just moved me in a new direction—a better direction."

"You should know Ezra is the one with the past. He changed his name and was previously charged with theft," I interject.

"I'm honestly not surprised," Gregory says. "Actually, I'm surprised there isn't more."

"Did you ever witness anything to make you think that?"

"I wish I had," he admits. "But it's more based on a feeling I always had. When I first met him, I thought he'd be a perfect addition to the church. He had the right ideals, a sense of family, and he also had the presence we were looking for. Then one day things started to shift. Example, I did not like asking for money from parishioners. I preferred to hold fundraisers for the church or take unsolicited donations. Without my permission, Ezra sent around a donation bucket during the service. He claimed it was to help a sick friend within the church who wished to remain anonymous. When I approached him about it, he wouldn't say who the person was, but my suspicion was that there wasn't anyone."

"Do you know what he did with the money?"

"That's the thing," Gregory said. "One day several hundred dollars disappear from the church's bank account. My guess, it was a test to see if he could get away with it. Not long after was when I lost my position. I assumed once I was gone, there wouldn't be anyone left to question where the money actually went."

"I'm sure his board and staff are aware of his dealings."

"Most likely," Gregory agrees. "And I'm sure there's a reason why they keep those dealings to themselves."

"Would you be willing, if we had the right momentum, to go public with that story?"

"Yeah, and some others I have. I'm not sure what good it'll do. It's all conjecture."

"It does the same thing Ezra did to you—it plants a seed of doubt. As long as we can draw some attention to his character, we're doing well."

"Do you have anything more concrete?" he asks.

"Not yet, but I'm hopeful," John says. "The way we've been moving lately, we're bound to find something soon."

"Good. That's good to hear. I'll dig up some of my old files and records from those days if the two of you want to take some copies with you."

We follow him through the church and into his office. I'm surprised when he drops in the middle of the room and pulls back the rug, rather than going to one of the filing cabinets perched against the walls.

He runs his fingers along the cracks in the wood, before settling on a spot and lifting several planks back. Beneath is a large, black safe.

He glances at us. I know I've got a bewildered look on my face. This was the last thing I expected.

"You've got to take precautions in this industry," he explains to us. But then he leans back on his haunches and scratches his head. "Well, others might not—but I do. Not just because of the Ezras of the world, but because there are others out there who have hidden agendas. I usually take notes about people—not in front of them, but after my meetings. I don't do it to be spiteful or rude. Just that I talk to so many people about so many problems and I can't always keep it straight. Pastors basically function as religious, low-salaried psychiatrists." He motions toward the safe. "I started doing this after a P.I. broke into my office. He was hired by a man who suspected his wife was cheating on him. They thought she would have confessed the affair to me and that I would have some sort of proof. I learned a lesson that day."

As he finishes the story, he starts rifling through his safe. Eventually he procures one of the thicker files labeled "Cain." He chuckles as he points to us. "I thought this code name was pretty clever."

I snort. "It's better than anything I'd come up with." I take the folder and start looking through it. "Wow, this is great."

"Good," he answers. "'Cause I've got more in the basement."

CHAPTER 16

Kinley

By the time we've gone through all of Gregory's records, we have three boxes full of documents. None of it will really help with what we're trying to do, but it does add context—bank statements, board meeting notes, sermon transcripts, and registries. The one board meeting that would've been good to have notes on was the one where they ousted Gregory, but that one is mysteriously not in his collection. I'm not surprised.

I honestly didn't know about the lie Ezra had spun about him. The thought of it made me sick. I can't imagine spinning a lie when the truth is so heartbreaking. I'm sure that marriage was a hard memory for Gregory to revisit, but Ezra didn't care. He was dragging them up and forcing the situation to be even worse for Gregory.

"Thank you so much again, Gregory," John says as we both put on our coats. He's going to go move his car, then come back inside so we can carry the boxes.

"It's really my honor," Gregory tells him. "I only wish I could offer more help. But please keep in touch with me."

"We will," John and I both promise. John reaches for

my hand, squeezes it, then says, "I'll be right back."

"Okay," I say, watching his back as he leaves.

When he's gone, I awkwardly finish buttoning my coat, fumbling. Gregory has been watching me closely since we started going through the boxes, which has me uncomfortable. There's this feeling of something unsaid weighing in the air between us.

He clears his throat, then says, "You're his daughter, aren't you?"

My gaze jumps to his, my heart sinking. "How do you … I don't …"

"When I came by your house after I got word from the board, I saw you sitting up on the landing, watching us. At first I thought you were Prudence, but then I saw"—he pauses and points to his cheek—"your scar. Ezra never mentioned he had a second daughter, but I assumed he did that day. I can see the likeness between the two of you."

"Nobody knows," I tell him quietly.

"I'm sure you haven't led a happy life."

"No," I say, feeling small. I wrap my arms around my middle.

"So you're honestly against him? This isn't a trick?"

"I can't keep letting him ruin people's lives," I tell him in a rush. "I have to make it stop."

"But John doesn't know you're an Abel?"

I shake my head. "I don't know how to tell him."

"You should. You're the biggest ammunition he's got."

"I know. I'm just scared."

"I think that's warranted."

"I'll tell him eventually."

"If you need to talk about it, I'm here," he says. "I can see you're trying to do good, and I'll be in your corner."

"Thank you," I whisper.

The door behind me opens and I jump. John walks in and I immediately wrap an arm around him. "Everything okay?" he asks, brow furrowing.

I force myself to smile and count to three—enough

time to hopefully get myself composed. "Yes. Just tired. Are you ready?"

"I am if you are." I'm relieved when his attention moves to Gregory. "We'll grab the boxes and get out of your hair." He gives him a quick handshake, then picks up two of the boxes.

Gregory shakes my hand, too, offering a kind, encouraging smile. I can't quite meet his eyes. That would feel too wrong because it should've been John to know first. I realize that now.

The truth has to come out, and it has to come from me. I'll give us tonight, but after the church service tomorrow, I'll tell him everything. It's time.

#

"We might freeze our asses off, but at least we'll have a good time doing it," John tells me as he squeezes my hand while we wait in line for hot chocolate.

We just finished dinner at a fancy restaurant on the levy above a river and now we're getting ready to walk along the aisle of small businesses. Hot chocolate, of course, was mandatory. Or at least, that's what John muttered when we came out of the restaurant to find the temperature had dropped.

The area is busy with couples and families, all enjoying the wintery scene. It's lit by streetlights built to look like old-fashioned, flame-lit lamps. It makes the light snowfall feel mystical—as if we're inside a snow globe. The buildings are also meant to look older, although they're clearly new, just representing an older colonial style.

"The hot chocolate will help," I promise, reminding him of his own words.

"With an avalanche-sized amount of marshmallows, don't forget that part," he jokes.

"How could I forget that? But what about the peppermint stick you mentioned?"

"Hey, hey, now, don't confuse my words. I said, *if it were Christmas, I'd demand a peppermint stick in my drink, too.*"

"We're getting here two months too late," I conclude.

"We won't make that mistake again when we come here during the holidays next year."

My heart flips as I hope against all odds that we do get to do that next year. More than anything I want him to accept me for who I am instead of my name. I'm not ready for this to end. The truth is, I think I love him.

John tangles one of his gloved hands in my hair as he presses a kiss against my lips.

"You're looking at me like you like me," he says, pulling away.

"I am," I agree.

"Like it's more than like."

"It is," I admit, but leave it at that. My realization isn't something I'm ready to declare anytime soon. Until I'm honest with him, my feelings can't matter. I can't let them get in the way of the truth. If I'm going to love him—truly love him—the very first step is for me to be honest with him.

"Yeah?" he says, giving me a wry grin. "Same here."

It's a weird conversation of single-syllable words and I wish I had more time to go back and understand exactly what both of us are saying, because I think I know, but it's hard for me to believe. I didn't realize somebody could feel this way about me.

I don't have time to think too much about it, because the man at the window is motioning us forward, then asking for our order. A second later, two steaming cups of hot chocolate are handed through the window to us.

I automatically blow on mine as we walk away, while John fishes one of his gloves off and into his coat pocket so he can pick out each marshmallow to eat individually.

I must give him a weird look because he demands, "What?" with a grin.

"You look like a kid right now."

"This is the *only* way to enjoy the marshmallows. You can't drink them."

"Do you realize how many opinions you have about hot chocolate?" I ask.

He laughs. "When you're family is in the food industry, you take any and every meal-slash-beverage seriously."

"Do you mind if I ask something?"

"I seriously don't mind anything you do, Kin. Although, I have a feeling you're about to sound like you got abducted by Althea." He leads us over to the levee overlooking the river. He leans against the railing, forearms on the top bar, cup clutched between his hands, and tilts his head to look at me. "Ask away."

"You didn't mention the diner in your dreams for the future."

"Noticed that, huh?" He glances out at the water, the noise of the soothing current and the happy voices behind us filling his silence. "I love Velma's, and I enjoy helping out where I can, but I don't think I want to pick up the baton when Tonnie retires. It's never something that's been in my cards."

"So I guess Tonnie knows?"

"Yeah. She gets it—me. I think it's because we're so much alike. She loves cooking and she enjoys the social aspects, but she had other goals in life. She wanted to go visit other countries and learn their cuisine, but Velma asked her to stay here and she did. Then when she passed … Tonnie wasn't going to sell the last thing she had left of her sister. So when I told her I didn't want the place, she understood."

"It's good you don't have that pressure from her," I say.

He nods. "I consider myself lucky. I mean, if she did expect me to take the place over, I would without any qualms. I love her too much to say no to a request like that."

"I'm sure she knows that," I tell him.

He pops the last few of his marshmallows in his mouth. "Yeah, and I'm glad it's enough. Some people expect too much of you—not for good reasons, either. As sweet as Velma was, she left the diner to Tonnie because she wanted her legacy to live on, not because it's what Tonnie wanted."

"That was very unfair of her," I agree.

"But I guess Tonnie could've been more honest. Velma knew she had other ambitions, but Tonnie never said that the diner definitely wasn't one of them."

"Did you know Velma fairly well?"

"I wish I knew her better," he answers. "If you're serious about looking into your biological parents, I'll help you. I really want you to give you everything you've ever dreamed of."

"Thank you for that. I would love to, but I think I'll need time to get the courage to learn about them. What if I don't like what I find? What if my real family isn't any better than my adopted one? For now, I've got you, Tonnie, and Althea, and that's all I need."

"But is it all you want?"

I take a minute to think it over. "Yes, it's all I want. What I have now is more than I ever dreamed I could have, let alone want."

"You're allowed to want more, you know. Courage or no courage."

"I was never in a place where I could. Give me time and maybe that'll change."

He swallows and rubs a hand over his face. "Kinley, I have so many questions about you and your past. I know you're hiding things … and that's fine. But I don't know how much longer I can go without wanting—needing—to know more."

"I know, and I really appreciate your patience." I bite the inside of my cheek. "I'm sorry I can't tell you more. Believe me, I want to. But I'm afraid of that, too."

"There's isn't a thing you can tell me that would scare

me off," he assures me with more honesty than my conscious can handle. *I wish you knew how wrong you are.* "I know how you feel. I was afraid I would scare you off, too. The path I'm on is a lot to stomach. Sometimes even I question it."

"You're trying to do good by people. In fact, you're trying to do *the best* thing I've ever witnessed anyone do. I move closer to him, until we're so close beside each other, we're touching. We sit there for a long time. Eventually he takes my hand in his and traces the outlines of my fingers. "I think Tonnie was lying when she said you aren't very social. You opened up to me in ways nobody else ever would or could."

I just wish I had the strength and the courage to do the same.

"Not about everything," he reminds me.

"No, but you did in time. You brought me into your life as a stranger."

"Now you're more than that." He leans to lay his chin on my shoulder and presses a soft kiss against my temple. "I wasn't in the best place. I forgot who I was and that I've got a purpose bigger than Ezra. Thanks for bringing me back into the world."

I close my eyes, then whisper, "Thank you for giving me a life."

#

Our hotel room is nice, with one giant king-sized bed, a TV, and a small sitting area. One wall is maroon, while the others are tan-colored. As John sets our things down, I walk across the room and sit on the bed, bouncing from the impact.

"I don't think I've ever stayed in a hotel before," I tell him.

"You're not missing out on much, although these are the nice ones." He scratches his jaw, checks his phone, and then sets it on the nightstand. When he sits down beside me, with his thigh barely touching mine, my cheeks heat with anticipation. *Nervous* anticipation. "Breakfast is good, too."

"Is it?" I ask, half-listening.

He makes a noise in agreement, then slips out of his coat and unties his shoes. "Tonnie can be cheap, so whenever we've traveled together, we always stay at those budget places. I thought you probably deserved better." He looks at me finally, winking. "Maybe just a little—hey, you look a little pale?" He brings a hand up to my face, rubbing his thumb along my lower lip. "Somethin' bothering you?"

I shake my head, at a loss for words.

"Did you want two beds? I figured since we usually sleep in the same—"

I answer his consideration with a kiss, cupping my hands on either side of his face and leaning into him. I hope he feels the words *I love you* in the kiss, even though I can't say them aloud. I want to say them to him more than I've ever wanted to do anything in my life—but saying them before any sort of a resolution to my lies is unforgivable.

"There's my answer, huh?" he says, pulling away so only our foreheads touch. We're both breathing heavier than normal. This is a chaste kiss compared to the others, but it's a prelude to what comes next. "How about we get this coat off you?"

I nod, absolutely lost as to how buttons and zippers work. Luckily, John's hair dances over my coat, undoing the button then dragging down the zipper. Even though there's still a layer of clothes, beneath the maneuver is overtly sexual. He pushes the coat over my shoulders and down my arms, then pushes it off the bed. He stands and steps in front of me. He tangles his hands in my hair at the nape of my neck and leans in, gaze vigilant. I hold my breath out of fear any movement will bring this speeding to a halt.

"Is this what you want?" he asks me. "You're doing this for yourself and not for me, right?"

"Yes," I say, but quickly realize that's not an answer at all. But at the same time, maybe it is. I'm doing this for the both of us. I want us both to have this. "I've never been this happy or so sure. I want to be with you, John."

He stares at me a second longer, waiting for me to contradict myself, but when I don't, he makes a low noise at the back of his throat and leans into me. His lips find mine, this time deep and searching—almost in a panic, not just to be with me but to be a part of me.

He pushes me back lightly and I fall backward with another bounce. We both laugh before clashing together for another kiss. Time is lost as our lips and tongues mingle in a long luscious tango, tasting of hot chocolate. I'm completely incapable of thinking about anything outside of this moment—hours could pass and I wouldn't question it. Time is suspended, and it's just him and me and *this*.

It's easy to love John and even easier to want to make love to him. This is an easy decision. It's the *only* decision I'll ever make that feels right, despite the circumstances.

He moves his hand beneath my sweater, tracing along my ribs. My body automatically arches into him, wanting his hand to move up further. I gasp something—not really his name or a word or even a thought—when his fingers finally find the material of my bra, tempting and teasing.

"Is this okay?" he breathes in my ear.

"Yes," I tell him. "It's all okay. I promise."

"Is that my cue to stop asking?"

"If I change my mind, I'll tell you."

"God, you're perfect, Kinley. You're my missing piece."

With that, his lips return to mine and he cups my breast. My body begs for contact from his, pushing my stomach and pelvis against him. I claw my hands at his shoulders, eventually sliding down to his waist and up his shirt, feeling the strong muscles in his back.

When he expertly slides his fingers beneath my bra, I moan into his mouth. Synapses seem to fire inside John, because his hips jolt against mine. I'm in a haze as he pulls me up with him to take off my sweater, then his. He starts kissing me again as he unlatches my bra. It falls between us, already forgotten.

He leans me back into bed, lips moving from mine and down my neck toward my breast. His tongue races along my scarred nipple, while his hand tugs at the other. I tangle my hands in his hair, pulling him closer. But somehow, despite how wonderful it feels, I want him to return to my mouth. I feel guilty that he's making me feel so wonderful, with nothing to make him feel good, too.

But before I can think too far, he uses his free hand to tug both my tights and panties down. A fleeting moment of fear washes over me as I realize he'll *really* see me naked, but it disappears as he kisses his way down my stomach, then down one of my legs behind my disappearing tights.

After my leggings are gone, he makes eye contact with me as he lifts each of my legs up and over a shoulder.

"Are you doing okay?" he asks

"Yes," I say breathlessly.

"Good. I like making you feel good, Kin." He leans over me and presses a soft kiss against my core. The muscles into my stomach tighten and I jolt, lightening spreading throughout my body. "It makes me feel good, too."

His tongue darts out, spreading me open, and then he kisses me there. Deep. Taking his time and using a talent and technique that surpasses anything I ever thought possible. My hands grip the sheets, pelvis arching toward him.

I don't think it can get any better, but then he adds a finger, thoroughly working me over. I yell louder than I want to—especially in the hotel room—but I can't help it. It's too good to keep quiet over. I would scream to the heavens about his ability if I could.

My heart starts beating at a thunderous pace, my muscles tightening and my mind going light. An intense pressure rises throughout my body, followed by warmth and then ... and then release shines bright. I feel weightless and heavy and heated and chilled and whole and empty all at the same time. It's so much that my eyes fall closed and I can't think or feel for several minutes. It's not until I hear a crinkly wrapper that I open my eyes and finally come back to reality.

John climbs onto the bed and lays beside me. He pulls my side against his chest, arm wrapped over my stomach. I can feel him hot and needy against my hip, but he doesn't push me further.

"You look so beautiful right now," he says. "You always look beautiful, though." His lips part against my scar and I believe him. "If I had met you before the church, I'd have religion. You're a ... goddess, and saying that makes me feel a little dumb."

I trace my fingers along his face. "You're not dumb. That was the sweetest thing you've ever said."

"I'm not much of a line guy," he tells me.

"I'm glad. I love you the way you are." I don't mean to say the *love* word, but I do, even if it's not an *I love you*. Thankfully, he doesn't read too much into it. Instead, he begins kissing me again.

Neither of us moves for a long time, instead only kissing. It's relaxing since I know (and sort of don't know) what's coming next. Eventually he traces the length of my body, teasing and tempting me with what's to come. Our contact becomes more frantic, both of us wanting more from the other. Need overpowers any nerves.

Before long, he's hovering above me, poised at my entrance. His gaze meets mine for one final confirmation before his hips push slowly against mine. A sharp pain follows the movement. A few tears escape with the pain, but it ebbs as he remains inside me, completely still. I rub his back when the pain is finally only a dull memory.

"It doesn't hurt now."

"No?" he says. "You promise? I don't want to hurt you any more than that."

"I feel great," I answer. "Amazing, actually."

He pulls back and grins. "Good. Because you feel amazing—I want you so bad."

Despite his words, he does as he was doing before. He kisses me to sidetrack my thoughts—maybe even empty my brain of everything. Regardless, it's impossible not to notice when he pulls out slightly and my body arches with him. The movement makes me feel the same euphoria as before.

I want him. I want him. I want him. It's a chant inside my head that is mixed with the other three words I can't say aloud.

Our bodies dance together in a wild tango of give and take until we're both sweating and moaning, clawing at each other to try to get closer. An orgasm rises inside me, pulling me closer toward the edge as John's thrusts increase in tempo.

Just as I start to fall again, his body presses into mine for one final hard thrust and he grunts into my neck. After what feels like an eternity of bliss, he pulls out of me and disposes of his condom. When he comes back, he pulls me back against his chest and kisses my mass of messy hair.

"You're the best thing that's ever happened to me," he whispers. "You're the most important thing in my life."

He says it with an awestruck tone and my heart aches. If I'm the most important thing to him, I have the potential to hurt him more than losing his family, Ezra, or anything else ever has. I might be his missing piece, but I could also be the piece that destroys him.

CHAPTER 17

John

I'm too busy enjoying lying in bed with Kinley's head on my bare chest, my fingers tangled in her hair as she sleeps. Having her here, although it makes my body want her, calms my head and makes it easier to doze off. But the truth is, the last thing I want to do is sleep when she's around. I enjoy looking at her—feeling her here with me—because I'm afraid she'll slip away. I can't bring myself to look away from her. Sometimes she doesn't seem real.

Last night didn't feel real. It was a moment far beyond anything I've ever experienced—anything I've ever dreamed of. Kinley gave me her body, but by God, I gave her my soul. Spending the rest of my life happy and with her felt within reach. She's enough for me, even above the church and Ezra and myself.

I should've told her the truth about my feelings, because right now, as relaxed and contented as I feel, I also feel guilty. My whole body is aching to tell her I'm madly in love with her. Despite the ache, I fight the urge to wake her up and tell her. I want those words to come with a moment as special and momentous as what she gave me last night.

My phone buzzes lightly from my nightstand, signaling a text. I want to just ignore it. I'd give anything to just hide away in this moment forever or at least until she wakes up. But nothing good is happening at six o'clock on a Sunday morning.

I have a sinking suspicion before I even look at the message that it's not going to be from Tonnie. I almost wish it was her. I'd take a fire or a robbery or anything over a text from Prudence. Well, that's a little extreme.

Prudence: Come to church this morning and I'll show you something that will change everything. Don't tell or bring your lying girlfriend.

This could just be some crazy set-up to get her clutches into me. But whatever it is, it could be a game-changer. Maybe I'll do what she asks and not mention anything to Kinley *today,* but I will tell her later about whatever it is Prudence is up to.

Me: Why do you suddenly want to help?

Prudence: I'm not helping. I'm keeping my word about being honest. I'm going to tell you the truth about everything.

Kinley lets out a long breath, her body tensing then relaxing. I quickly turn my phone off, but she's already pulling away from me to lay her head on her pillow and look at me.

"Why are you awake?" she asks with a sleepy smile, not even bothering to ask about my phone or my general weirdness.

I set my phone back on the table then roll over to face her. "Just didn't want to fall asleep with you in my arms. Felt sacrilegious."

"I'll still be here when you wake up, you know," she tells me. "I'm not going anywhere."

"I know you're right, but I'm not used to keeping people in my life other than Tonnie. Usually they either pass away or … they can't handle the church taking up so much of my time."

"There've been a lot of women who've left you because of that?"

I give her a half-smile, more embarrassed than anything. "I don't think *right here* is where we should be talking about that."

"It's really fine. I want to know."

"There haven't been *a lot*. A few women I've tried dating, but not in the past year. The last one did a number on me. Not because I loved her, but more because she laid down some truths I had to face." I lay my hand on hers, which earns me an encouraging smile. Here I am talking about other women and there's no jealousy whatsoever. "I decided at that point I wasn't going to see anyone until I had put all of this behind me. But then you came along. Honestly, you mean so much to me that if you asked me to, I'd give all of this up. Ezra, the church—everything."

Something flashes over her face. A sadness. "I would never ask you to do that."

"I know, but if you did … you're the only person I've ever felt this way for." I use my other hand to scratch at my jaw. Given the drive back and then having to get to the church service, I won't have time to shave. I guess I probably need to get us moving, no matter how much I hate that. "I got a text before that the station needs me, so we should start heading home soon."

She pulls the blanket with her as she sits up, careful not to show anything. I might have already seen her completely naked, but there's still some hidden mystery between us. As if every experience with her will always feel new.

"I should probably be getting home too. But that thing I wanted to talk about?" She pulls her lip nervously between her teeth. "Can we do that tonight? Please?"

"Yes, of course."

She lets out a breath. "Good."

#

Luckily, by the time we got home, I had enough time to see Kinley off and change into my "Sunday" wear. God, I hated leaving her and knowing I was lying to her. I could tell she knew something was up, too. But she's too good of a person to ask about anything. She'll give me time to tell her everything. I will in time, but it's the deceit until then that's been sitting in my stomach like rancid trash since Prudence's text.

About a half-hour ago I got another one from her, telling me to go in *after* the service starts. Her directions were to use some keys she was going to leave in the drawer of the table the sign-in book is on, then go around the back to the outside stairs. I didn't even realize there was a door back there, because of the trees surrounding the building.

As soon as I've got the keys in hand, I realize where she's leading me to—that control room. From there, I'll know all the ways Ezra works to fool his congregants. But why's she showing me that? Is she doing this for her own nefarious reasons or because of Ezra's? Even if she is doing this to show me she's honest, then what's her motive behind all of this? She's not just doing it out of the kindness of her heart. She's not that kind of person.

The outside stairs at the back of the church are concrete and lead up to a door with cracked, white paint. I shove the key in, half expecting alarms to go off. This could be a setup.

If that's the case, then I really don't know how I'll explain any of this to Tonnie and Kinley. I'll need one of them to bail my ass out of jail.

Nothing happens as I unlock and open the door to a bland, white-walled room with one door and an open doorway to an office space. It's dark in there, but I'll bet that anything within reach is locked up tight. Even behind a locked door, I doubt Ezra would leave anything to chance.

As quietly as I can, I walk to the door and open it.

I'm right; it's a control room with dated TV screens for viewing live-camera footage, a lighting and soundboard, plus a one-way mirror hidden so well I've never noticed it. But somehow none of it matters, because sitting in the chair like she's the great and powerful Oz is Kinley.

I stumble back, feeling as if someone's rammed their fist through my chest to squeeze my heart. There's a giant lump in my throat the size of a meteor. Hell, I feel as if I've been hit by one of those, too.

Prudence was telling the truth about her.

I can hardly believe it. Maybe she was set up? Maybe she's just trying to get more information just as I am. Maybe …

She swivels around quickly, her face drained of color. "John," she says. My name barely makes its way out.

"What are you—tell me this isn't what it looks like, Kinley."

"I—" That's it.

I stare at her, all of the hopes I'd had draining away along with any semblance of trust I had. I thought we were in this together. I thought she was mine—that we belonged together. But all this time, she's been on *his* side. No wonder why she seemed to know everything.

I turn but immediately run into Prudence. The number two of this little scheme. She's grinning from ear to ear, arms crossed, the same mixture of plain and perfect as her sister. The same. … *evil.*

"See, I *always* tell the truth." Prudence feigns sweetness, but it's sickeningly sweet—nails on a chalkboard. "But Kinley, here, she doesn't. Do you, Kinley?"

"Prudence," Kinley says in a pleading rush. "Why are you doing this?"

"Because someone has to. Someone had to tell John your dirty little secret, didn't they? How long did you honestly think you would get away with this?"

"I was going to tell you," Kinley says, standing and stepping past Prudence toward me. Her hands come out, like she's going to reach for me, but then she drops them. "John, I wasn't. … this isn't …"

I swallow, anger boiling. "How exactly do you fit into all of this?" I demand, jaw clenched. My eyes are burning. All my feelings, though, are numb. Of everything that's ever happened to me, this is the one I don't want to feel. I won't be able to work through it.

Kinley doesn't answer, but instead continues mumbling nonsensical syllables.

"C'mon, sweetheart, put two and two together," Prudence says to me.

"I want to hear it from her."

Tears are streaming down Kinley's cheeks, but I refuse to buy into it. She's such a great liar, I could've sworn she really did love me back. Now I know I can't trust her actions.

I can tell she's not even going to tell me the truth right now.

Prudence goes ahead and answers for her. "She's Ezra's other daughter—my sister. He's been pulling the strings the entire time."

Kinley shakes her head. "No, John—no—you have to listen—please—"

I can't listen to her or her sister anymore. I have to leave—get away from her and this damn church. *Her* church.

It's all poison.

CHAPTER 18

Kinley

Tears are pouring down my cheeks as the door slams behind John.

I almost can't believe that less than a moment ago, he was standing in front of me with so much hate in eyes— hate toward me. I knew that one day he would find out … but when I decided that *I* would tell him the truth, I didn't expect him to react this way.

I expected many different reactions and they all played throughout my mind during the service. John being empathic toward my upbringing, wanting to work things out. John deciding he could never forgive me, and John leaving me.

None of them included hate. I was being hopeful and naïve. If I had been honest with myself, I would have realized that hatred was the most likely response. How could he not hate me?

My family ruined his.

I'm the enemy.

No matter how much I tried to help, I wasn't doing anything productive, because I was withholding my truth.

"That was dramatic," Prudence says in a sing-song voice.

I spin toward her, hair smacking against my cheeks. I'm equally as furious with her as I am myself. "Why did you just do that?"

She looks at her nails, hand on her hip. "Because it was necessary."

"It was necessary?" I yell. "What about that was necessary?"

"You weren't accomplishing anything." She narrows her eyes. "You were *helping* him. He was going to ruin everything."

I hold my arms out. "This place needs to be ruined. The church *hurts* people, Prudence. It ruins them."

"So?" Her face contorts. "Nobody ever cared about us and whether our lives were being ruined. Nobody cared when we were being shuffled around foster homes. Nobody cared when Ezra used us. Why should I care about anybody? Why should I not use this place to my advantage?"

I angrily bat away my tears. "Because that's an evil thing to do. Mom and Dad would have wanted us to be good people."

In a cool voice, she kills me her next words: "Mom and Dad are dead, so who gives a shit what they think."

I don't have time to recognize what I'm about to do until I've charged toward her and slapped her. Her hand immediately goes up to nurse her cheek, and her jaw tightens.

"Don't ever speak like that again," I warn her.

Her eyes narrow. "If Mom and Dad wanted to do good by us, they would've put a will together."

"They couldn't have known what would happen to them!" I exclaim, turning and walking away, afraid I might hit her again.

"I don't care!" Prudence yells back. "They died and we were alone! We had *no one*. There wasn't anyone to love us or take care of us. Nobody *wanted* to. Doesn't that make you angry? Why shouldn't we show people as much disrespect as we've been shown?"

I face her again. "It does make me angry. I don't want to care about anyone or anything. I *wish* I could care less like Ezra. But I don't, and that's because I love you, and then I met John and I fell in love with him, then his family…"

"He can't love you, Kinley. He doesn't know you."

"Well, now he does." I close my eyes and squeeze my fists at my side. "How could you do this to me, Prudence? Do you really hate me that much?"

I open my eyes to meet her blank stare. "Yes."

I barely hold myself together. "I have done nothing but love you. I've protected you as much as I could, I've taken your abuse, I've hurt John to protect you—"

"Who. The. Hell. Cares." Each of her words is punctuated with a sharpness that seems to pierce my heart. "You might think you've protected me, but you haven't. Nothing that you ever did mattered. Ezra still whored me out, demanded I do cruel things, treated me like a plague. *You* were up here—hidden away and just doing the soft touches. *I* was down there—I broke people's dreams and forced them to lie and fed into their fears. *I'm* the one with the black on my soul. Sure, he used you in the beginning— but what was that? Petty theft?" She throws her arms. "You've been useless to me my entire life. I wasn't going to let you get your happy ending."

I draw in a sharp breath. "But what about yours, Prudence?" I demand. As much as what she's saying hurts and is probably true, I still have to believe that there is goodness in her. "What about your happy ending?"

She laughs without humor. "My happy ending is here. I'm rich and I stand to inherit a whole church-full of people willing to give up their time, money, and service."

"You can't be this evil. I know you aren't."

"I am," she says, and shoulder-checks me as she walks

by. "And judging by John's face, you are, too."

When she's gone, I fall on the floor. I fall to pieces. Her words are all too real. I am alone. There's nobody here to help—nobody to pick me up and put me back together.

CHAPTER 19

John

Kinley doesn't get the message that I want to be alone, so I take the option away from her by turning off my phone. If she comes over in person, she'll get the same response. Her betrayal burns too strongly to face.

How did I not see the damn signs?

I thought she wasn't forthcoming with her past because she was embarrassed or because it was difficult. But I should've known there was more to it. The same with how I should've known it was weird that she lived so close to the church and always miraculously had information. Not to mention how easily she entered my life, then took it by storm. It was so easy to fall in love with her, and now I know it's because it was all orchestrated.

No matter how real it felt—no matter how real my feelings are—it's all based on a lie.

I mean, she even fooled me into believing she and Prudence didn't know each other. Looking back, I thought she was afraid of Prudence, but really she was afraid of Prudence ruining everything. Their acting was so good, I even missed the resemblance. How they have the same button nose—how they share the same smile. But they both use them in different ways. Kinley's to seem kind and innocent, Prudence to be heartening or to seduce.

This whole time Kinley's been the one orchestrating the effects. I can barely begin to wrap my mind around it all. Because worse than anything is the fact that she's not just a part of that disgusting church—it's that she's Ezra Abel's *daughter,* adopted or not.

Somehow I had to go and fall in love with a monster's daughter. I don't want to face that part. It's easier to think about being duped. I don't feel so … ended.

Demolished.

Somebody starts knocking on the door with the same loudness and fury as my growing headache is. Clancy is clearly so freaked out that she stays where she is on the floor by my feet. She's been cowering since I came home, all while I've been shifting between a daze and rage for the last few hours.

"John, open this door!" It's Tonnie.

My body refuses to move. I'd like to just stay here for the rest of my life. What other types of hell are out there waiting for me?

"John, open the damn door. I know you're in there," she says. "What the hell is going on? Why does Kinley keep calling me and the diner?"

Great, she's moved on. I get up, body lethargic as I move to open the door. Clancy stays where she is, making a small whining sound.

"There you are," Tonnie says, as soon as I open the door. "I was worried—what's wrong? Why do you look like that?"

I rub my hand down my face. I must be bordering a panic attack because my head feels light and I feel as if I could fall right over if the wind hit me.

"John," she says. Her hand comes out to squeeze my arm. "Talk to me."

I'm not embarrassed to say that when she opens her

arms, I take her up on her offer. She's almost half my size and I'm a grown-ass man, but it's moments like this one when a man needs a mother-figure. Somebody to lean on when his whole world is basically ending.

By the time I've composed myself, Clancy is whining and Tonnie's patience is growing thin.

"What's going on?" she asks, leading me over to the couch.

"She's one of them. Kinley's one of them."

"She's one of who?"

"The church. She's his daughter. Kinley fucking *Abel.*" Her last name comes from my lips as a growl. I think I'm more furious at myself because no matter how mad I am, I can't turn off my feelings. I drop my head in my hands. "God, Tonnie, I *love* her. I—I don't know how I'm going to get through this."

The last words don't mean anything to Tonnie. She's clearly too focused on the first part. "She's Ezra Abel's child."

"Her and her sister were adopted," I say mechanically. "I only thought he had one."

"Why would she do that to us? To you?"

"Because he told her to."

"But what's the point? It'll only make you hate that church more."

I don't say anything.

"John, tell me you're still in this."

All I can do is drop my hands and slam my palm into my fist. Clancy barks beside me then runs off to the safety of her bathroom. "He knew if I had feelings for her I wouldn't be able to shut his shit down."

"But she doesn't love …"

"You think I don't know that, Tonnie?" I snap. "Of course she doesn't love me. Of course she never cared or wanted to know me. It was all a part of their little scheme. The only problem is that it doesn't change how *I* feel. I can't keep going after the church after what she meant to me."

There's a ridiculously stupid shred of hope that I can't help but believe that maybe I did mean something to her, too. Everything else might've been fake, but last night was real. She gave me a piece of herself that she's never given anyone else—and that's not just something a conniving person does. If it was, I wouldn't be her first. She wouldn't have looked at me the way she did or reacted the way she did when I touched her …

But the smart majority of me sees her sitting in that chair, fooling people—people like my family and Althea—into thinking there's one last glimmer of hope.

"I'm sorry for my tone, Tonnie," I apologize. "I just don't see how I'm going to move forward after this."

"You'll figure out a way. You always do," she assures me.

I nod, but I don't agree. "It's all just so different with Kinley. Losing her …"

"I think we're both too shocked right now to sort through anything," she says. "But the Kinley we knew was sweet and easy to love. It's going to take time to sort that out against who you've found out she really is."

"It doesn't feel right," I tell her. "None of it feels right. But it's the truth. I could see it in her eyes."

"How did you find out?"

"Prudence," I answer. Somehow, when all is said and done, I'm not that pissed at Prudence. Sure, she's pure evil, but she's honest. No matter what, I always knew I stood on scorched earth when it came to her. But with Kinley, it's the opposite. I can't be sure of anything, because nothing was ever real with her. "She said she had something to prove she wasn't a liar. I hoped she was talking about Ezra, but I should've known. She never was going to want to take him down—her interest was all in destroying Kinley. There's no such thing as a sisterly bond there. Out of everything Kinley said, the parts about her sister were the truest."

"At least we now know the reason for Prudence's crude message."

"I think she could've found a better medium," I say.

"Clearly she has a flair for the dramatic."

"Look at who raised her," I say then add, the pit growing in my stomach, "and Kinley."

"So you really are going to stop just because your heart got involved and now it's all a mess?"

"I don't know." I sound exhausted even to my own ears. Exasperated.

"Nothing's changed."

"*Everything's* changed."

"Okay, so you got involved with the wrong girl, but don't let that ruin what you've worked toward. We're in this to stop *Ezra*. We're here because *Ezra* made a promise he couldn't keep. We're here to protect people from *Ezra*. And no matter what, we're doing this for others. We're in this to help all parties move on and to make it so no one else can be hurt the way we were. This is beyond you and Kinley."

I suddenly feel as if I'm a teenager and Tonnie's teaching me an important lesson, which is exactly what she's doing. I need to hear it. Everything she's saying is the absolute truth. I'd be selfish to give up now, just when I'm starting to make progress.

"You're right," I admit. "Just give me a couple of days to sort myself out, then we'll get back in this thing."

She nods, proud of herself. "Okay, good."

"This has got me feeling like I've been run over by a cement truck."

"Nothing a couple of drinks with your favorite aunt won't fix."

#

I'm only buzzed, but Tonnie and I still take a cab to and from the bar. But judging by my slow recall and my suddenly clumsy body, I'm not meant for more than two drinks. At least I made those two drinks count because, while all that hurt and betrayal is still running pretty strong, it's been numbed. I won't be charging the Bastille anytime soon, that's for sure.

Tonnie, though, has the tolerance of a whiskey barrel. There's a reason why the first and only time—up until now—that I've gone drinking with her was for my twenty-first. For such a tiny lady, she can drink the best under the table and not even feel it. Case in point, halfway through the night, she started talking about a new marketing strategy she's going to use for the diner. At least Althea's been good for her.

Tonnie gives me a quick hug before she heads across the street toward the diner. I scratch at my head, wondering if she'll even wake up with a headache. I'll definitely have one. Maybe not from the alcohol, but definitely from the stress.

I hear Clancy barking before I'm even on my floor, which has to be driving my neighbors crazy. I really need to invest in some sort of My Dog from Hell training for her when it comes to barking. I'm sure Althea would count that as a dream for what comes *after,* right?

As soon I can see my door, I freeze in my tracks. Kinley is sitting with her back against it, arms wrapped around her legs. For the first time since I've met her, her hair is pulled up so her scar is completely on display. She's also wearing a pair of sweatpants and a T-shirt that are both two sizes too big. When she looks at me—meeting my gaze so I'm staring into her red-rimmed, tear-filled eyes—I decide it's time to walk.

I carefully ignore her, even going so far as to slip my key in to unlock the door. "John," she says just as softly as the subtle click.

My muscles tense, any positive effect of the alcohol had gone. Now all I've got left is the lethargy and exhaustion. Plus the beginning tremors of a headache.

"I don't want to do this, Kinley," I say, leaning my head against the door. I'm too tired to keep ignoring her or try arguing with her.

"I know," she says quietly, searching for my hands. I'd be lying if I said the unexpected warmth didn't make my heart speed up. Somehow she's become a need I didn't realize I required almost as much as eating, sleeping, and breathing. *Damn you,* heart. "I'm so sorry to have put you through all of this. But will you please let me talk to you? I promise that's all I'll ever ask of you again."

I swallow. "Did any of this mean anything to you?"

She stands, moving close to me. There's urgency in her actions and her voice. "Yes, of course. You mean *everything* to me. I just ... I've never had to choose between my life and anything else before. I didn't know what to do."

I step away from her and turn the knob to open my door. I want it clear that there needs to be space between us. "You can come in."

She lets out a small, relieved sigh and follows in behind me. Clancy stopped barking at the sound of my voice, but she still seems uneasy as she darts forward to give Kinley the once-over. She's lost all trust in Kinley, too.

I head straight for my Keurig and start brewing myself a coffee. I need something to keep me going for this conversation.

Kinley stands listlessly in the middle of my apartment, Clancy now just watching her.

"I'm so sorry, John," she says, then starts crying.

I believe her tears are real, but I don't budge from my spot. The part of my heart that hasn't realized we're no longer in a good place wants to comfort her, while the other knows the best place for me right now is to be detached. To listen. To observe.

But this is another example of how I don't really know her. I didn't think she cried. Everything she's ever told me, she's said without any tears—including the tough stuff.

My coffee finishes and I throw away my pod. "Do you

want any coffee?" I ask, voice even.

She nods, rubbing at her eyes. I fix her up what she likes, then put it down on the island when it's finished. Watching me, she takes the seat in front of the coffee. I stay where I am, leaning against the counter.

"Where should I start?" she asks.

"Wherever you think you need to."

She nods, taking a sip of the coffee. "Ezra liked to threaten me by using Prudence. I did everything he said because I wanted to protect her and I didn't want to be separated from her. But I also had to stand by while Ezra made her do things, too, and eventually she changed. She used to hate him and wanted to escape as much I did. He originally wanted to send Prudence to you to … well, you know. I couldn't stand the idea of her getting involved, so I made up excuses so he'd send me instead. I think she was angry—jealous."

"Given her actions, I agree," I say.

Kinley offers me a sad smile. "I'm so sorry for the damage she caused. If you would have known her when she was younger—she was bright, and she loved to use her flair for the dramatic to make me laugh."

That's hard to picture, but I don't tell her that. Instead, I cross my arms. "None of this explains why you didn't tell me Ezra was your father."

"I should've told you," she says quietly.

"Yeah, but you didn't."

"I wanted to, and I was planning to tell you, but I didn't know how. I fell in love with you, John, and I was terrified if I told you, I'd lose you."

"You *lost* me, Kinley, because you *didn't* tell me." I pause to take a drink of my coffee, if only to calm myself down. "If you would've told me in the beginning, I might've had my reservations, but I would've trusted you. I can't trust you now—not after this."

"I might've not told you about my family, but I promise that everything I've been doing and the way I feel about you is one hundred percent real."

"That doesn't change the fact that all I needed was your honesty. I needed the truth *from you*."

"I wish I could go back and tell you everything."

"That can't be done."

She brushes a new tear away from her cheek. "Is there anything I can do?"

I shake my head, words lost in my throat.

Her face falls, paling, and she shifts off her seat, giving up on her coffee. "I love you, John. If there's one honest thing I've ever said to you, it's that. If you change your mind, no matter how long that takes, I want another chance to help you learn to love me back again. The real, honest me." She lets out a long, shaky breath. "Ezra is aware of what's happened between us, but he doesn't know anything else. The group should be safe to continue on."

She leaves me. Just as the door shuts, Clancy changes her mind about her animosity toward Kinley and runs after her, whining. I feel close to doing the same thing.

CHAPTER 20

Kinley

When I get home from John's apartment, my things are scattered across the porch. Ezra is waiting for me, leaning with his back against one of the porch spindles and his arms crossed. He has a stern look on his face. To anyone else, he might look like a father angry with his daughter for breaking curfew.

"You followed my request too well," he tells me.

I sigh. My eyes are dry of tears, and I don't care about pretending anymore. "You request too much of everybody and expect too little of yourself."

He works his jaw. "Excuse me?"

My shoulders drop as I reach for one of my bags and sling it over my shoulder. "I've been afraid of you for my entire life, but I didn't realize until today how it is to be truly afraid. I mean, you're nowhere near as intimidating as Prudence."

"You aren't allowed to speak to me that way."

"What are my consequences?"

He stares at me.

I open my arms and motion to my bags. "This is *all* I

have left. You can't threaten to take anything away from me. I've already lost Prudence and John. What else is there?"

"There's still a lot you can stand to lose," he threatens. A fire that wasn't there before lights in his eyes. It takes all my composure not to flinch. "How about those times when you were younger? When you *willingly* begged strangers for money? When you *stole* from them?"

"I was a child under your influence," I tell him.

"People don't know that. And all it really takes is for me to bring to light a few instances in the church's history where you might be culpable for fraud. Like the money that went missing and was put into an offshore account under your name."

Chills run over my skin. "What are you talking about?"

He only smiles.

"You're blackmailing me for something *you* did, aren't you?"

"I'm not doing anything except protecting my family."

"No, you're protecting *yourself*. You've never cared about any of us—not even Michelle."

"It's not like you've cared, either." He turns, ready to go back inside. "If we ever hear anything from you again—if you even reach out to your sister—the information is released."

#

I sit at the bus stop in town with my bags for hours, unsure of what to do next or where to go. I can't begin to think how to solve the problem, because I just keep seeing John's expression. He was so ... he was broken, and I did that to him. He said I couldn't have really loved him, and maybe he's right—if you love someone, you don't hurt them the way I hurt him. Even though I thought I loved him, maybe there's something wrong with me, and I *can't* love him.

Everything feels completely and totally … hopeless.

I really thought I was going to do the right thing. I thought I was going to fix everything wrong that Ezra's ever done by helping to bring him down. Mostly, I was convinced I'd found my purpose. But now … now I don't have anything.

"Don't feel sorry for yourself," I mutter. "This is all your fault, anyway."

But it's not even that I feel sorry for myself. I *hate* myself.

My phone starts to ring, Althea's name popping up. She probably found out the truth and now it's her turn to voice her anger. I answer, because I know she deserves that chance.

"Hello?"

"Oh, thank God. There you are, Kinley. I've been calling you for hours."

I pull my phone away to look. Sure enough, there are a lot of missed calls from her. I guess I've just been thinking so deeply that I haven't heard anything. "Sorry, I didn't hear the phone ringing."

"Where are you?"

"I'm waiting on a bus."

"Don't wait on a bus. Let me come pick you up."

"Althea, hasn't Tonnie or John called you?"

"Yes."

"And you know?" I ask. My voice cracks.

"Yes. Where are you, Kinley?"

I answer her, but I don't understand how she can know and still want to see me. "Tonnie, Ezra is my father. I lied to everyone. Aren't you ma—"

"Kinley, dear, I am not mad. Now stay there and we will talk once I've picked you up."

#

Althea didn't lie to me. She doesn't seem mad in the

slightest. But she doesn't let me talk, even after we've gotten back to her home. Instead, she insists I change into pajamas and join her on her couch for milk and cookies. I do as she says, but when the glass is in my hands and cookies are resting on my thigh, my eyes prick with tears and I cough at my suddenly scratchy throat.

"Drink the cold milk and get some sweets in you, Kinley," she orders.

I nibble on my cookie.

"Good girl. A little food will help." She is in her pajamas, too, although her top and bottoms have little sheep in hats on them, which is way trendier than what I'm wearing. "Tonnie called me a few hours ago and she was understandably upset. At first, I could understand it—I was upset also. But then I realized that you might have lied—but that doesn't make you a bad person. Neither does having a monster as your adopted father. In fact, despite that, you are a *good* person. Maybe I haven't known you for very long, but I can see you have a kind heart. You deserve to be heard out and understood."

I look at her, eyes wide. I feel like a little girl. As if knowing this, Althea scoots closer and twines her hand with mine. The tears officially fall, but words also tumble out. I basically tell her my life story, beginning with my adoption, leading into the way Ezra used me, and what happened with John.

When I finally finish, she pulls me into a long, comforting hug. *Is that what it's like to have a mom?*

We stay that way for a long time. It's nice to finally be honest with someone and to just let the truth settle between us. I know I need some time to let it percolate, and I think she does, too, no matter how strong she's being for me. No matter what she thinks of me, I'm tied to the people who wronged her family. I'm complicit in their actions.

After a while, she squeezes me one final time and pulls away, leveling her gaze with mine. "Kinley, sweetheart, you've been involved in some terrible things, and I know that you've caused a lot of heartache along the way, but anyone who was not raised by that evil man has no right to judge you. You were captive to his demands as his adopted daughter, then broken into submission to keep your sister safe. You were not going to win that situation."

"How are you not angry with me?"

"Because we are all only human." Althea points to a picture of her husband. "Before we were married, I didn't trust men. My dad had a drug addiction and left me in many situations where drugs were clearly more important to him than I was. Parents shape us into the people we become. We don't even realize it until someone or something changes our life. John was what you needed to change yours, just like my husband changed mine." She cups my cheeks now, emphasizing her next words. "But hear me, even if you started to change because of him, you're the one who has and will put in the work. Now, you're changing for *yourself,* which is where good health and happiness begins. My dad made me into a sad, untrusting person, but *I became* a strong, successful, joyful woman. I see the same situation in you."

I can only stare at her, wanting to believe she really thinks that way, but also wondering if she's being honest with herself. What if she changes her mind?

"I can see you need time to think about all of that," she says. "Learning to love yourself is hard."

"Do you think John will ever forgive me?" I sound both hopeful and pitiful.

"I don't think it matters what John does. I think the only person who should matter right now is you. Can you forgive yourself?"

"I-I don't know."

"Then that's where you need to start," she tells me. "It's where we all need to start."

CHAPTER 21

John

Three Months Later

I'm prepared for it when I walk over to the diner to grab a cup of coffee and some breakfast before I head out for my shift at the radio station, but seeing it is still weird.

Almost an out-of-body experience—something I didn't ever expect to see in my lifetime.

Velma's up for sale.

When Tonnie told me her plans to sell the diner and do some traveling, I was more than happy for her. I agreed with her decision because I knew it was the right one for her. She has enough in her savings to get by, and she deserves to enjoy herself. She's always wanted to see the world, so I'm glad she's finally going to be able to do that. It'll be strange not having this place in the family, but it'll be for the better. I think we both just need ... space.

Not from each other—but from the life we've made for ourselves.

Ever since the fallout with Kinley, I've put some distance between me and the church. That helped me realize that I don't have a lot to my life outside of that, the diner and my dog. I would honestly say I don't have much of a life at all. It says a lot if Kinley was the one and *only* bright spot in it. Losing her sent me into a tailspin of loneliness, but I also had this really cliché opportunity to find out who I really am.

The first thing I did was stop attending the church services. Sure, I still plan on taking them down, but I can't ruin myself in the meantime. I've reserved one day a week for research days, while the others are about catching up with myself. I've been taking Clancy on hikes, watching documentaries on Netflix, and going for runs. For the first time in my life, I've got my mental health in check.

I also asked my producer at WJWJ if I could switch over to a day show. She wasn't a huge fan of the timing of my request and told me no at first. Then a week ago, one of the day-people put in their two weeks' notice. Evidently they decided to try their hand at podcasts. I also got a raise out of it, which is not something I expected.

"What in the world are you standing out in the cold for?" Tonnie demands as she opens the door and ushers me in. "You're making my customers nervous."

"Sorry—just taking in the new decoration," I admit, motioning toward the handwritten sign.

She looks at it, as if just noticing it's there. "It's my handwriting, isn't it? It took you off guard? Maybe I should've just printed it."

"No, no, it looks fine, Tonnie. It's just strange."

"Just about you and everyone else has said that to me today. This is the right thing to do, right?"

"It's the right thing," I tell her, then pull the door open wider so I can walk in. She gives me a look as I pass, like she's some sort of a human lie detector. "Honest," I promise. "We've all just got to get used to it is all."

"I think I'll miss the people, but I won't miss getting up at five in the morning." She points to my usual spot in the back. "I've got you all ready to go."

"Thanks," I say and make my way over.

I half want to move somewhere else. It's damned hard sitting in this booth without Kinley across from me. I still can't find it in my heart to forgive her, but I regret not giving myself the chance to try. I shouldn't have blocked her out of my life the way I did. I was just so hurt—when I looked at her, I saw Ezra pulling the puppet strings. I thought I was in love with *her,* but really it was just the shadow she was casting.

How would I even begin to fall for her again? The trust wouldn't be there, and I don't know if I could talk myself into taking the chance again. It took me that long to open up to someone—to *love* someone.

I set my fork down and take a long drink of my coffee, wishing it was something stronger. Just as I'm setting my mug down, somebody slides into the seat across from me. My eyebrows automatically raise when I realize it's Althea. I called her shortly after the whole thing with Kinley went down and she was furious. Only she wasn't furious with Kinley.

Imagine being that man's daughter? Imagine he's who you have to depend on? What would you do?

We haven't talked since she chewed me out, then hung up. I should've guessed she wouldn't be mad at Kinley. They had a special bond. I wouldn't be surprised if Althea knew, even before I did. Something about that thought, though, makes my vision blur and my heart harden. I don't want to think about her confiding in someone else when I was always willing and there.

She sets her forearms on the table, jewelry clanking, and gives me a serious look. One eyebrow raised, lips in a tight frown. She's wearing a navy blue suit with a white shirt underneath.

She's the one who's angry with me, even though I don't return the feelings. "Hi, Althea."

Her frown deepens. "I'm here to ask you to come with me."

I'd be honest if I didn't immediately worry about the

next location of my body. "Where?"

"The news station."

I choke on air. "The news station?" I repeat.

She only stares at me.

"Why are we going there?"

"Because, thanks to you, Kinley doesn't think there's anything left for her to do except tell everyone. I had a contact at the station and I set it up, *reluctantly*." She points a long, manicured fingernail at me. "This is going to ruin that poor girl. As if she hadn't risked everything already, now she's going to have a reputation."

"I don't understand. What is she going to do?"

"She's going on the five o'clock news to do a tell-all about the church."

My heart drops. "No, she can't. If she goes public—"

"That's what I've already told her, but she *wants* to. She thinks she's making up for everything she's done. Except that poor girl hasn't done anything except follow the rules to provide for her sister. She's a victim in all of this, but people like you treat her as if she's to blame."

"I don't mean to—"

"You can try to talk me out of being disappointed in you later. For now, we need to go show her support. Lord knows she's going to need it."

#

There's a crowd of people outside of the new station, all clearly from the church. They have signs protesting Kinley's segment, most of them calling her a liar. There's one in particular that makes my blood curdle because it says, *Let the rest of her burn.* I've never been a violent person, but I'd really like to take that sign to the person's head of who came up with it. I'm even pissed they'd call her liar.

God, as mad as I was, I'm not anymore. Somewhere in the last month it faded and it was just stupid pride holding me back from her.

"Great, the vultures are here," Althea mutters as she shows a badge to the security station. The man motions for her to keep going. "I don't know how the church found out."

"They've always got an ear to the ground." I glance at the clock on her dash. "Think we've got time to stop her?"

"You know we won't be able to stop her. We have to let her do this."

I argue with her in my mind instead of out loud. Even if Althea was wrong, I wouldn't be able to dissuade her. Clearly, she's been influencing Kinley to be the same way.

She parks toward the top of the garage, then quickly leads me toward an elevator, which we take to the lobby. The perky, blond man behind the table informs us where we need to go and reminds us to be quiet. He emphasizes this with a finger in front of his lips.

His directions take us to a sound booth, where Kinley can be seen but not approached.

She's on the other side of the glass, but she feels miles away. Was this how she felt at all those services? Contained? Trapped?

She looks completely different, wearing a black dress, with her blonde hair perfectly curled and her face caked with makeup. I'm guessing Althea dressed her, then the makeup department here took things a step further. She's a completely different person. I wonder if this is the real Kinley Abel—the one I didn't have the chance to know. But then she smiles shyly at something the female reporter is saying, I see her—*my* Kinley. Maybe she's all one and the same, I've only just seen one side of the coin.

She's sitting at a large, wooden desk opposite of a brunette with a tight red sweater and pearls.

"—If you're comfortable, that is," the reporter finishes.

"Natalie's asking about Kinley's childhood," one of the producers whispers.

Kinley's nervous smile makes sense now. Her hands fidget in her lap as she struggles to maintain eye contact with the reporter. "It was … it wasn't what a childhood should be. Ezra used me. He liked the fact that my scar made me seem weak and helpless. He liked to put me on street corners without a jacket and make me beg for money. When he started working for the church, he stopped making me the center of attention and started hiding me away." She tucks her hair behind her ear, drawing attention to her scar. "He thought people would judge him for not healing me."

I swallow, doing my damnedest not to picture a younger Kinley begging. Trying not to picture her cold, innocent, and malleable.

"What did you do for him instead?"

"I did a lot of the behind-the-scenes work. I controlled all of the effects we used to … trick people."

"Why did you do that?"

"Because I had to," she says quietly. "He's a man on a mountain of threats. He's already told me if I speak out, like I am today, he's wired some funds to make it appear as if I've been embezzling from the church. He mostly used my sister against me. For the longest time he refused to adopt her, too, unless I helped him."

She tried to tell me that, but I believed there had to be more at the time. I mean, why would she want to protect Prudence?

Because Prudence is a victim of circumstance, too. She couldn't have always been bad.

"Now, I know most people will take your word for it. But some of our viewers still want evidence. I'm told you brought something today that might serve that purpose?"

Kinley pales but nods. "Yes."

"And what did you bring?"

She stutters. "Ezra's notes."

My heart stops. "How did she get those?" I ask— demand. "She didn't …"

"Break in?" Althea offers. "No."

"Then what?"

Suddenly I notice another woman standing off to the side of the set—Michelle. She's just as dressed up as Kinley, only her clothes hang off of her. Even from here I can see she's shaking, somehow paler than Kinley. *Deathly* pale. She's holding a binder in her hand, marked with brightly colored labels.

She walks onto the stage, nearly tripping over herself. But she gains the same stoicism, with her pleasantly blank expression as she, Kinley, and the reporter start going through the documents. From one of the production crew's TVs, I can see where they've got a blown-up version of the documents on one-half of the screen for viewers to see. Clear as day is a measure of Ezra's wealth, as well as notes on the people he's scammed and how he's done it. There's also notes on the congregants—talking about which ones would make good plants—but their names have been redacted on the screen.

"Kinley's been staying with me since Ezra kicked her out," Althea explains quietly so she's not bothering the staff. "Michelle contacted her a few days afterward. She wanted to leave Ezra. Kinley and I helped her escape one day during a service, then we checked her into rehab. She's been staying with us for a few days now."

"Why did she decide to do that now? You don't think she's the one who tipped off Ezra's people, do you?"

Althea shakes her head. "No. She was drowning under Ezra's control. Plus, it's clear she loves Kinley."

"None of this makes any sense," I say.

Althea only pats me on the shoulder. "It's because you wouldn't *let* it make sense. There's more to the story than right and wrong. But you defined the line and wouldn't bend. Kinley's not bad or good, she's somewhere in between—although I think she is mostly good. We all have our faults."

By the end of the interview, it's not clear whether Ezra will face repercussions from the law, but I know for a fact that any sort of following he's gathered will be ruined.

Nobody is going to trust him after this. The evidence shows he's a cruel, narcissistic man who's no more a God than me.

The reporter offers Kinley and Michelle a handshake, saying a few more words while Althea and I make our way out of the booth and toward the set.

Kinley might've been nervous before, but at the sight of me, it worsens. I can tell because her breath catches and she wraps her arms around her waist. She offers me a shaky smile.

The two of them walk over to us and Althea immediately greets them both with hugs. "You both were wonderful," she tells them. "I'm glad I made it back in time."

"Me, too," Kinley says. "I didn't know where you went to."

She won't look at me, and I don't have the words to ask her to.

"John needed to be here," Althea tells her. "What you did was big, and I didn't want you to have to do it without him. Why don't we all go downstairs to the lobby? There's a cafe down there where you two can talk."

"Okay," Kinley agrees. Michelle only smiles. I'm too muddled to do anything except follow them.

Luckily the cafe downstairs is empty, with only a bored barista as our audience. She takes all of our orders and fills them quickly. Before we separate, Michelle straightens and turns to look at me. Now that I think about, I've never actually interacted with her. I've only seen her from afar, with those glassy eyes and dazed expressions. Up close and sober, she's younger than I thought. She might've just been a kid herself when she took Kinley and Prudence on to raise.

"John, I want to apologize for what my family did to you," she says. Her voice is shaky. "You did not deserve it."

I don't know what to say. Even though I'm ready to

move on, I can't forget. Michelle might've been trapped or high most of the time, but she was still complicit. She *chose* that lifestyle and chose to lose herself in it, rather than escape. I'm glad she finally did—and that's what'll redeem her to me. But it'll take time to get to that point.

I nod briskly. She smiles. There's a lot more to say, but an awkward encounter is enough for now. Stepping stones.

"Do you want to take a walk?" I ask Kinley.

"Okay, yeah," she says.

"We'll be here when you're done," Althea tells the both of us.

Kinley and I head outside, coffees in hand. The news station is in the middle of a city, a far cry from the small towns we've walked through together before. The tall buildings and other pedestrians make me feel very insignificant. Honestly, I guess I've *been* feeling that way. Look at what Kinley did—it's amazing. But what did I really do for the cause? Here I was blaming her, but really it was an excuse to step back.

"I'm sorry," I blurt.

Kinley's gaze is focused on the sidewalk. "I know. I am, too."

"You shouldn't be, Kin. As much as I don't want to admit it, you were right not to tell me about your dad. I don't think I would've given you the time of day."

"You might've eventually."

"Maybe, but you don't deserve to be treated like that. And you *really* didn't deserve my anger once I found out. Hearing you talk today … Kinley, I didn't realize how bad it was for you. I should've known." I pause, then let out a long, pent-up breath. "I need to tell you something. I love—"

Kinley's face whips in my direction and she stops walking. I do, too, and turn toward her. "Don't say it, John. Please don't say it. The truth is, we don't really know each other. You can't love me because you haven't met the *real* me."

"Sure I have."

"You've met a version I made up."

"You might've made up your history, but I know you. I know that you laugh when you're dreaming, that you like to pet Clancy's nose, that you think more than you talk, that when you look at me your eyes sparkle. Where you were born and how you were raised doesn't matter to any of it."

"I always thought I was better than Ezra but, honestly, I'm not. I can see that now. If I wasn't under his thumb, I wouldn't have lied to you for so long. I have to unlearn everything about my life that Ezra and the church taught me." She lets out a breath and tucks her hair behind her ear. "I want you to love the real me, John."

"But I already—"

"You might think you do, and you might be right. I just want us to slow down and reflect and think about what we really want. I think we need time."

"Apart?" I ask. The word literally hurts.

She bites her lip. "No, not apart. Losing you hurt too bad—I never thought you'd forgive me. I just want some time to get to know each other. To fall in love without anything hidden between us."

"That's fair. But, Kinley, I'm already sure of my feelings, and I'm going to prove them to you."

CHAPTER 22

Kinley

Five Months Later

The shockwave after my interview was nightmarish. I knew it would be, but I wasn't prepared for it.

Althea keeps saying it's the nature of PR. "There are always the three schools of thought on any given subject—for, against, middle. People in the middle either don't know what they believe or they just don't care. To get through this, focus on yourself and what you believe," were her words after one particularly trying day. Even though you'd think what I said would be enough to bring clarity to Ezra's followers, there are still a few who believe in him. A few of them harassed me on a date night with John; they called me terrible names and warned me I'd burn in hell.

Most people are on my side, especially since Ezra effectively ran off with his tail between his legs. He didn't even try to fight. If I had known it would be that easy, I would've taken him down sooner. The few who aren't on my side are loud and terrifying. All I've ever wanted was to feel normal, but now I feel even less normal than ever.

Luckily, it's all finally starting to slow down. I don't have as many random run-ins or angry phone calls as I did in the beginning. There were also jokes about me being the "cult-girl" on the internet, but that's died away. And the people who thought I could help them with their cult-like situations haven't been trying to get a hold of me as fervently as they once were.

I figure I had to get through an extreme abundance of abnormal to find normalcy.

Until then, I'm trying to do what I can to help the situation. I started working at a library shortly after the interview, which I really enjoy. I feel very at home there. Nobody seems to care that I have a weird past, a scar on my face, or that I'm a little behind on what's happening in the world. They just accept me for me. It's refreshing.

I've also found a fondness for taking Clancy on long walks, journaling, and watching all the television shows and movies I've missed out on. I'm also excited because last week, as a surprise, John got me subscription to genealogy database. For the first time in my life, I can learn about my parents and my family's history. It's both daunting and exciting to know where Prudence and I came from.

Althea has also been helping me study to get my GED. I want to apply to college. It goes to show how wrapped up I was in the church—I didn't even realize how important it is to have a high school degree. It's something I would've had to consider if I ever escaped the Church of Life, but I guess it's also a privilege I never noticed. Under Ezra—even though he threatened to take it all away—I didn't have to worry about an education or expenses. As long as I did as he wanted, I was taken care of.

It was all at the expense of my happiness. Now that I'm working and being productive, I feel like a different person—a happier, lighter person.

Even going into the situation I am right now, I feel positive. John squeezes my hand, as if he senses I'm thinking about what we're going to do. I smile up at him and lean my head against his arm for a split second.

I'm about to see Prudence for the first time since she exposed the truth about me to John. Since she's still only seventeen, Michelle used her parental authority to have her signed into a psychiatric hospital. The doctors there have been working with Prudence to get her the help she needs. They've made progress toward changing her way of thinking—helping her to realize that Ezra's way of life was wrong. They also diagnosed her with a Narcissistic Personality Disorder, which they've been treating. A mixture of a devastating past, difficult upbringing and her disorder created the perfect storm that made Prudence seem like a lost cause.

But she's not, I remind myself. I do feel guilty because I should've recognized there was another issue. I should've worked harder to find a way to put both her *and* John first.

"Did they say when she'll get released?" John asks.

"She turns eighteen in a week, so I think they're more worried she'll check herself out. I think if she doesn't, they're going to keep her longer," I explain. We're walking through the parking lot to the hospital, which is expansive and homey. We were very lucky because the hospital decided to work with Prudence pro bono so long as they get to use her case as a study.

"Let's hope she chooses to stay."

"I have a feeling she will. She must be responding pretty well to her sessions and treatment." I look up at John, still in awe that he chose to stay with me. "I just hope she can find something similar to what I have."

John took me very seriously—he started taking me on dates, treating our relationship like the beginning of something rather than the middle.

On our first date, John took me to dinner at an Italian restaurant. Althea helped me shop for a pretty outfit and she did my makeup—evidently Tonnie also bought John a new outfit. The date was awkward at first—especially because we had gone so long without speaking and there was so much scorched earth between us. The awkwardness faded, however, when John finally opened his mouth and started asking me questions, one right after another.

What's your favorite color?

What books do you like to read?

Have you seen any great movies lately?

If you had to do one thing for the rest of your life, what would it be?

The questions got odder and more random until he finally slowed down and explained, "I wanted to have the chance to ask you everything I've always wondered."

I wish he would've asked me those sooner. I'm sure he had others back when we first met, but at least these were answerable. I hate that he believed I was so closed off, that he could not ask me anything as simple as my favorite color.

On our second date, he took me to a fair. I had never been to one before, so we ate a lot of fried foods and other oddities, and rode nearly all of the rides. I felt more carefree than I ever had. I felt like I was experiencing a piece of childhood that I'd missed, and I grasped onto that. I wanted to remember that feeling for the rest of my life.

On our sixth date, we ate a picnic lunch in his apartment—we were supposed to go outside, but it had rained. I decided it was time to tell him everything I had held back about Ezra, the church, and my upbringing. While I was speaking, he guided my head toward his lap and rubbed my temples. Clancy laid with me. It was nice not to have to look at him, because it made my words flow better amongst the tears.

Eventually he took me back to the place we'd gone when he bought me the hot chocolate. We relieved that night and its memories and he told me he loved me. It was the first time I let him since he found out the truth, as well as the first time since I'd met him that I believed him. He knew the truth and I knew that meant he could really, truly love me.

We've told each other we love one another everyday—every hour—maybe every minute—since then. Our beginning has been rewritten. It isn't marred by Ezra's poisonous lifestyle or my lies.

And now I'm getting a fresh chance with my sister, too.

When we enter the hospital, we're asked to wait so a nurse can walk us to Prudence's room. John pulls me against his chest and kisses my head. "Nervous?"

"A little. I hope she wants to see me."

"I'm sure she does. If she's really changing for the better, she'll see you've always wanted the best for her. Honestly, I wouldn't blame you if *you* didn't want to see *her*."

"It's weird because, despite everything she's done, I still do. She's my little sister, and I'll love her no matter what. I might not *like* her, but I'll always love her."

"You're the best kind of person, Kinley," he says. "I'm sorry I forgot that for a time."

"Please don't keep apologizing for that. We were both wrong."

"I know. I just regret it. Guess I want you to know *how much* I regret it."

A nurse appears from behind a security door and shakes our hands. She gives us a quick overview of Prudence's health and current treatment, then tells us a few rules. After about five minutes, she leads us through a series of hallways, which are painted a warm brown. After what feels like a maze of walking, she stops at a door with Prudence's name written on a chalkboard.

She knocks, then opens the door to a surprisingly nice suite. There's a small kitchen, a twin-sized bed, and a little sitting area. The room is sparse, except for a few pictures hanging on the yellow walls. There's no TV or any other sort of technology; instead, they've given her a few books to read in her spare time. They're open and sprawled around the room—on her bedside table, on the coffee table, on the couch.

Prudence is awkwardly standing in the middle of the room, wearing a pair of black tights and a baggy sweatshirt with the hospital's logo on it. I've never seen her look so—normal. Her hair is just pulled back in a ponytail, she's wearing no makeup, and her feet are bare. Her hands are clasped in front of her as she smiles nervously at John and me.

She lifts a hand and waves it. "Hi, Kinley." She composes herself before saying, "Hi, John."

"Hi, Prudence," I say back, while John just nods. His hand is protectively nestled against my back. Probably ready to drag me out by the back of my shirt if Prudence gets confrontational.

"I'll leave the three of you alone. I will be down the hall if you need me," the nurse says before disappearing. I'm shocked that she would leave us alone. Don't we need a mediator or something?

"Do you want to sit down?" Prudence asks. She flashes a smile, which, thank goodness, is very authentic, because I would think she was just going through the motions otherwise. Her voice is very even and controlled, sounding like she's just following a script. What if she's still just pretending so she can get what she wants?

"Sounds like a good idea," John says. "Kinley?"

He motions for me to lead. I sit down on the two-person sofa and John sits next to me. Prudence takes the armchair adjacent to us. She's closer to me than John.

"So," John says, clearing his throat. "How've you been, Prudence?"

"Good. And you two?"

"Good," John says.

We sit in awkward silence. John's knee bounces up and down, while I stare at the coffee table in front of us. After a minute—just when I feel like I want to jump up and run—Prudence says, "I'm sorry."

My gaze jerks up. Her face is earnest. For the first time in my life, I see my sister as *pretty*. "Prudence …"

"I'm *really* sorry, Kinley. I don't know what happened to me. I was so mean to you, even though you always tried to give me the best. I know they said I have a … disorder, but I can't believe I was so cruel. The psychiatrists said that I couldn't help it—I was just coping—but I-I don't see how."

I tangle my hands in my lap. I want to hold hers—or John's. Something to ground me. "I forgive you."

"But—"

"If I don't forgive you for what's happened between us, it'll be unhealthy for the both of us. I want us both to be happy because neither of us have ever really been able to enjoy life. But you're also the only other person in the world who understands what it was like to be brought up in that environment. It's nice to have that."

She stares at me and then shakes her head. "You're too good of a person."

"I love you. You're my sister. I'll do anything for you."

"I know you will. You've always been here for me, even when I was terrible." She looks down at her knees. "I love you, too."

This time, I reach for her hand and squeeze it. "We're all going to get through this and come out on the other side."

"I really hope you're right." She glances at John and winces. "I'm sorry for the way I treated you, John. I was jealous of Kinley and I took it out on you."

"I know. It's all right. It all worked out. Might not have gone the way we'd have all wanted, but it all worked out in the end," John tells her.

"I've done so many bad things, and I don't know how to move past them," she whispers, teary again. "I slept with men and broke marriages and stole and …"

She starts to babble and every word she says hurts. I knew vaguely of the things she was doing, but I also tried to keep it out of my mind. I'm guilty for turning a blind eye. When she started to act out, I didn't try as hard to protect her. I stand and then squeeze onto the chair with her. I wrap my arms around her and pull her into me.

"Ezra is the reason you did all of those things. You were in those situations because of him."

"But I *enjoyed* doing those things, Kinley."

"It was your way of life and survival and the disorder. I bet in a few years if you were put in one of those situations, you wouldn't do it again. Just give yourself time to heal. You've already come so far."

"It just seems like a long way away. I wish I could be better right now—today. How were you able to move on so fast?" she asks.

"I'm still moving on. Just because I'm functioning, doesn't mean I'm better. I've been seeing a counselor, too, and sometimes John has to correct my way of thinking. Last week we attended John's company picnic and I had a panic attack in the bathroom in the middle of the event. I realize now I felt so uncomfortable in that situation because Ezra punished me if I was seen by a large group of people. I'm used to hiding myself away. And I was also self-conscious of my scar."

"Your scar makes you beautiful, Kinley," Prudence tells me. "It always has. But I think I needed to hear that. It makes me feel better."

"Good. I want you to know that you aren't alone."

"Thank you," she whispers. She hugs me tightly. "You have no idea how much I've needed this from you." She pulls back and her expression turns kind, eager, and bright—three things I never thought my sister was capable of. "Now, tell me things."

I laugh. "What things?"

She waves her hands in a wide motion. "*All* the things."

"That's a lot of things," I joke.

She tilts her head, feigning annoyance. "I'm serious."

"I don't know what you mean," I explain.

She lets out a sigh and wrings her hands, not meeting my gaze. "There's just so much I've missed out on and so much I don't know about you—and I want to know it all. I want us to be sisters and friends and … do all the silly things we missed out on because of Da … Ezra."

I don't know what to stay. I glance at John, but he just nods encouragingly as if to say *go on*. But I have no clue where *on* is. I want those things with Prudence also, except getting there is the problem. Forgiving her is easy, but forgetting? How can I truly trust her again? I love her more than my heart can bear, but what if my sister takes my heart and crushes it?

John is looking at me with love.

It's probably something stupid to realize. We tell each other how much we love one another more times a day than I can count. I *know* he loves me. He loves me despite the lies and betrayal. Despite my past. Despite my blood. I gave him my heart and he gave me mine, and even if we hurt each other, our hearts mended and we found our way back to each other.

I can do that with my sister—I *will* do that.

Closing my eyes, I breathe out through my nose and then I rehash everything over the last few months—up to and including what I ate for breakfast this morning. It might take time, but if telling her "all the things" is what it takes to move forward with my sister, then I will do that and more.

EPILOGUE

Kinley

Seven Years Later

"Kathleen McKinley Smith, Master of Social Work."

The words coming from the speaker's mouth feel random and unreal, even though I've strived toward them for the past seven years of my life. It started with my bachelor in social work, which I was able to do in a fast three and a half years, thanks to scholarships, my part-time job at the library, and lots of hard work (and tears).

During that, I also worked on coming up with my own thoughts and perspectives—I finally started thinking as myself as a whole and as Kathleen McKinley Abel, rather than just Kinley. I'd been a shell of a person, shaped by Ezra and the Church and my own fears. I only afforded myself one name, one shadow, one path. But now, I'm more.

Then I traded Abel for Smith, one of the *best* decisions of my life. I traded up in every sense. John and I chose to have a destination wedding on the beach, with only Tonnie, Althea, Michelle, and Prudence in attendance. Neither of us was interested in the fanfare—we only wanted to make our vows to each other. It was the first time in my life that I felt an authentic religion—a promise to a power higher than the two of us to always love, respect, and support the other.

After that, we welcomed a foster child into our lives—Mandy—then her younger brother, Danny. They've been in our family for about two and a half years now, which John and I are hoping to make permanent by adopting them. They're both wild and fun and so serious sometimes it hurts. Mandy is fifteen, meaning she's a slightly snarky teenager, but she's also a wonderful artist who makes sure she has every Thursday open to watch old movies with us and drink hot chocolate. Danny, twelve, has some behavioral problems, but he can make us laugh until our stomachs hurt, and he loves hugs. They remind me of Prudence and me—their parents died a few years ago and all they have is each other. It makes understanding them easier, but I would've loved them even if they had a completely different story. They're John and my kids—they've become our world and our hope for children to have a happy life, despite the bad pasts we've had.

It's amounted to today. Me in a graduation gown, about to receive another degree in profession I'm passionate about. My family is cheering loudly from the stands, causing warmth to spread throughout my heart and soul. My professors are smiling at me, because they supported me through my undergraduate career, followed by my graduate career (which took longer because of marriage, work, and kids). And there's a baby, a month away from meeting us, tumbling around in my stomach like he's in a bar brawl.

Of everything that's led me to this point, he's probably the part I have the most disbelief about. Not just because of the baby brain, but because I never thought I'd bring a child into this world. I didn't believe in myself as a mother, as a wife, or as a person. I didn't think that I deserved any of this. I didn't think that I meant enough to this world to bring another life into it. I thought I'd created too much negativity to welcome light.

But then John happened—followed by Tonnie, Althea, Mandy, and Danny—and now I feel whole. I feel like I can accept myself and everything else, including this baby.

I manage to waddle to the stage and take my degree without crying. But I don't follow the rest of the graduates back to my seat. Instead, I take a door and follow a little tunnel out of the arena. I got special permission to leave, so I wouldn't be stuck in my seat for several hours, feeling unhappily pregnant.

Somehow, everyone makes it outside before I do. Danny immediately runs toward me and wraps his arms around me and my gigantic belly. Everyone else crowds around me, alternating between congratulating me and asking about my health. I beam over the congratulations and wave off their worries.

"You're amazing," Prudence says over everybody else. She's been in school for business, but she's been doing a lot of acting in local theater. She's really got a flair for it, that's for sure. She hugs the side of me that Danny is currently not hugging. "I can't believe how cool you looked."

"You'll look just as cool when you're on that stage next year," I remind her.

"It's taken me long enough," she says. The GED and college haven't come as easily for Prudence as it did for me, but she's been working toward her own graduation steadily. On top of that, she's been improving her psyche and coping with a mental illness. I honestly find her so much more inspiring, because I know how much effort she's put into making a better life for herself. She's taken adversity and shown it the exit door.

"Don't be hard on yourself," Althea warns. "You're a strong ass woman just like Kinley."

Althea has taken Prudence on to raise, just as she has Michelle. They both still live with her, although Michelle has something like an apartment in the basement. Even though she's been an adult for far longer than Prudence and me, it's been really difficult for her to find her footing. I think it's because she was under Ezra's thumb for so long, plus her problems with substance abuse. She's been gradually working toward independence, but I also think she's happy just being her own woman. Sure, she depends on all of us a lot, but nobody tells her what to do or how to live. She doesn't say anything, which isn't unusual. She only smiles at me. She does much better one-on-one, which means she'll probably go with me to dinner as a celebration in a few weeks.

Althea, however, is thriving. She started her own business, has a steady boyfriend, and has been making speeches on grief. We all idolize her.

Then there's Tonnie, who's been traveling and finding herself. She comes home mainly for the big events, but that's fine because she's having the time of her life. I know John misses her, but it's easy to look beyond that when she's constantly sending pictures of her where she's beaming. She's almost gone backward in age; she's been so happy.

"I have celebratory drinks and dessert set up at your house," she tells John and me.

"When did you do that?" we ask almost at the same time.

She shrugs. "I'm a woman of mystery. Let's keep it that way."

"Thank you," I tell her.

"Anytime. Although, I'm sorry you can't enjoy the drinks. I learned how to make them from a tiny restaurant in Mexico. They're delicious."

"Why're you still talking about them, Tonnie? You're only rubbing it in." John laughs.

"Can I have a sip?" Mandy asks.

"No," John and I both say. Of course, Tonnie says otherwise. Luckily, Mandy knows we have the authority in the situation and pouts.

"Let's all head out and grab the cars. No use making Kinley walk," Althea says, then ushers everyone away to give John and me our space.

He produces a colorful bouquet of roses he'd been very sneakily hiding behind his back. I grin as I take them from him, but can't help myself. I wrap my arms around his waist and kiss the underside of his jaw. "They're beautiful. I love them—you."

"*You're* beautiful," he tells me. "And, even better than Prudence's *amazing,* you're perfect. You've wowed me in every way. You've got no idea how much I look up to you."

"Please. You're an amazing father, a hotshot radio personality, the best husband, and a catch. I'm a little obsessed with you."

He laughs. Then kisses me on the lips. Then kisses me again, deeper this time. I blush, even though there's no one around except for food vendors.

"Seriously, I'm proud of you, Kin. This is a big deal. You've already been doing great things, but I can't wait to see what you do next."

"I honestly can't either," I tell him.

"And then there's you, young sir," he says, putting his hand to my stomach.

"He's restless."

"He wants to say hi to us in person."

I bite my lip and place my hand over his. "I can't wait to give him the best life. I want him to have what we didn't have the chance to have. Not a perfect life, but a close-to-perfect one, with uncontrollable happiness and potential."

"He will. I know he will. I think we found each other because we were both missing something the other one had. But this boy will have the whole of us—he'll grow up knowing to appreciate his life and knowing that he has it *good.* He'll have two parents who love him, an entire extended family that adores him, and two siblings who pick on him as much as they protect him. He's going to have the best life."

I lay my head against his chest. "Thank you for giving me *my* best life. Everything was a mess, but then you happened."

"Then *you* happened," he says back. "Amazing isn't it? That we managed to find each other in such screwed-up circumstances?"

"It's a miracle," I murmur.

"Serious question." He pulls away from me and his gaze searches my face. "Are you ready to save the world, Mrs. Master of Social Work?"

I laugh, holding up the book they gave me that is meant to represent my degree. I do my best imitation of a power stance. "I was destined for this."

"Yeah you were," he says, clapping his hands together.

Tonnie parks the SUV in the circle beside where they left John and me.

Mandy leans out the window in the backseat. "You two are so embarrassing," Mandy declares, nervously surveying all of the (cute) college boys who aren't paying any attention to us. "What are you two even doing?"

John gives her a dorky look. More of his teeth show, his eyes widen, and his head jolts forward. It's what I call his "dad" look. He mainly does it whenever he wants to further embarrass the kids. "Your mother is celebrating."

"Does she have to do it like that?"

"I could kiss her instead ..." he threatens.

"Ew!" Danny immediately declares. Evidently, it is gross to see your parents show any kind of love toward each other—up to and including hugging—so we utilize that in every way possible.

Whether he's following through on his threat or not, John leans in for one final kiss before we leave. I lean my head against the passenger window and smile to myself as we drive home, the kids still complaining in the backseat.

I always wanted a family, but this is more. This is more

world, my love, my life.

ACKNOWLEDGEMENTS

First and foremost, there isn't a number of acknowledgments I can write or thank yous I can say to express my eternal gratitude to Melissa Keir and Inskpell Publishing. Thank you for taking a chance on a young writer and proving that wishing on stars can, in fact, work.

The same goes for the unbelievably talented Yezanira Venecia, whose keen eye and skillful editing made this story better; and Najla Qamber, who has a special ability to take a story you've put so much time, effort and love into, and create a beautiful cover that always reaches far beyond your expectations.

Finally, I could not have written this story without the eternal support of my parents and fiancé. Mom and Dad, you have no idea how much it means to me that you ask about my writing, create social media posts, and attend events with me. The two of you are the cheer squad every young woman needs in their life—without you, I wouldn't have the strength, courage, or perseverance that it takes to write and publish my work. Nathan—you don't know it, but you were one of the first people who heard me verbalize the idea for this story back when we first met. I wrote this in our beginnings and it will be published just after we're married. When we fell in love, you taught me how to love. I hope that this is evident in my writing from now on.

OTHER WORKS BY LIZ ASHLEE

Step Toward You
Sort of Normal

<u>Anthologies:</u>
Once Upon a Summer
Magic & Mischief

LIZ ASHLEE

CHECK OUT...ANOTHER BOOKS BY LIZ ASHLEE

Step One: We admitted we were powerless over alcohol-that our lives had become unmanageable.

There are twelve steps in Alcoholics Anonymous and Silas Manning knows all of them by heart. He's been living them since a drunk driving accident resulted in the destruction of three lives. When he meets Rooney Oliver, he quickly realizes you can be addicted to things other than alcohol—you can be addicted to people, too.

Rooney's mother is dying and Rooney feels like she's dying with her. It's not until Silas comes into their lives that any of them start feeling hope—but Silas isn't ready to let go of the past or open himself up to a future.

Sometimes the only person who you want to lose is yourself.

AVAILABLE IN EBOOK AND PRINT AT ALL MAJOR BOOK RETAILERS

Falling in love isn't as easy as staying in love.

Carter Hart and Boone Fell's lives are tangle of perfect and imperfect memories. In a world of drugs, alcoholism and neglectful parents, their love for each other kept them strong. But all it takes is one kiss and a lie to tear them apart.

When Carter's brother, Declan, dies of an overdose,

Boone decides he can't let another day of secrets and mistaken circumstances keep them apart. His only problem? Now that he's ready to move forward with Carter, she's ready to leave him where she thinks he belongs: in the past.

AVAILABLE IN EBOOK AND PRINT AT ALL MAJOR BOOK RETAILERS.

LIZ ASHLEE

ABOUT THE AUTHOR

Liz Ashlee is an avid romance reader and the author of *Step Toward You* and *Sort of Normal*. She recently earned her Master of Arts in English degree from Northern Kentucky, where she also earned her undergraduate degrees. Liz lives in Kentucky, where she loves spending time with her parents, fiancé, friends, dog, and cat.

Website: https://www.liz-ashlee.com/
Facebook: https://www.facebook.com/LizAshleeAuthor/
Instagram: https://www.instagram.com/lizashleeauthor/
Twitter: https://twitter.com/lizashleeauthor?lang=en